Whispers of a Man

Hamza Abdullah

2009

Whispers of a Man

The Story of Ancient America

Hamza Abdullah

This is a work of fiction. The events and characters described herein are imaginary and are not intended to refer to living persons. The opinions expressed in this manuscript are solely the opinions of the author and do not represent the opinions or thoughts of the publisher.

Whispers of a Man
The Story of Ancient America
All Rights Reserved
Copyright 2009

Cover Photo Copyright 2009 SXC. Used with permission. All rights reserved.

This book may not be reproduced, transmitted, or stored in whole or in part by any means, including graphic, electronic, or mechanical without express written consent of the publisher except in the case of brief quotations embodied in critical articles and reviews.

Ink House Press
http://www.inkhousepress.com

ISBN: 978-0-615-31352-8

Ink House Press and the "i" logo are trademarks belonging to Ink House Press.

PRINTED IN THE UNITED STATES OF AMERICA

Author: Hamza Abdullah
Typest and Layout: Hamza Abdullah
Cover Design: Hamza Abdullah
Web Site Design and Engineer: Hamza Abdullah

Dedication

*To Marwa, for whom I climb high mountains,
    And to "the people" who were lost but are now found.
    Hamzatu*

Prologue

Sometimes things are buried to be hidden from view and sometimes they are hidden to be found later. Buried under the feet of America lies the echo of the past that is whispering on the wind. That echo is the whisper of a man. A once great civilization walked the path that we now walk and left footprints for us to follow.

The past cast a powerful shadow that cannot stay ignored and forgotten. A debt must be paid so that the descendants of man can continue. This work is the result of listening to the whispers of a man echoing and is an attempt to wake up the sons and daughters who have forgotten and are now obfuscated. The whisper is telling all those who are confused, mislead, and bewildered that there was a time when they stood taller than any.

There was once a great civilization on the North American continent that could rival any that has ever existed. The ruins of the fabulous civilization lies buried beneath the soil of the land. Yet to even the untrained eye the evidence is obvious. There once existed a pyramid building and advanced civilization in what is now the United States of America proper. This civilization was contemporary with Egypt, Babylon, and India. As apart of the civilization that spanned the globe the Ancient American civilization was held in eminence around the world.

"Whispers of a Man" is the story of the highly evolved and advanced civilization of Ancient America. The clear evidence of its existence is calling to all so that what is hidden can be exposed to light. The evidence that exist calls to all indigenous and native Americans to re-recognize their past. In recognition of the ancient past lies the key to the self-resurrection of man.

Chapter 1

"The ground on which we stand is sacred ground. It is the blood of our ancestors." Chief Plenty Coups

This is a story about the story of man. What man? The original man. He walked on this land from long ago. And he is the same man who is walking on it today. Except he doesn't know that he is original. He thinks that he is a fake. Some time ago the original man was made into a carbon copy of himself. Now he is an obfuscated man. The original man is now a forgotten man.

"Momma! Rat and Duute done cut off my topknot," shouted Dump, who was sixteen, as loud as he could. He stood there rubbing the place where his hair used to be.

"Momma! They done put a big ole blacksnake down my shirt while I was sleeping," screamed Leroy who was seventeen and the oldest of ten children.

"Rat...Duute," Amanda called to those two.

Those two were nowhere to be seen. There was going to be a spanking for somebody tonight. Now if only they could catch them.

"Rat and Duute, yaw'll come on in now it's starting to rain."

The summer rain in southern Virginia smelled so sweet when it mixed with the fragrance of honeysuckle and roses. The long lazy days provided plenty of opportunity for two little ones to get into mischief. They didn't mean any harm when they stuck that snake down Leroy's shirt while he was sleeping under the Magnolia tree. And they thought it was just hilarious when they cut off Dump's topknot. They were laughing the whole time cause it was so much fun.

"Be quite Duute, momma going to whop us good if we go in

now. When it stops raining we'll run away and never come back," whispered Rat who was eight to her five year old little brother, Duute.

Hiding under that old box bush was the best hiding place in the whole wide world. Momma would never find them there. Not even the rain could touch them under that bush. That box bush was so big that it covered practically the whole front yard. It had to be the biggest box bush in all of Virginia, at least in Beasleytown.

"Come on Duute, let's run. Let's run far away."

The two made their dash as fast as they could. They ran as fast and as far as their legs could carry them. They got as far as Mister Johnson's house before it started to rain really hard. The thunder and lightning started to make Duute afraid.

"What yaw'll doing out in the rain?" Mister Johnson called from his front porch. The two little ones stood in front of Mister Johnson's house getting soaked from head to toe. The old man stood on the porch smiling.

"Come on up here out of the rain."

"Hi, Mister Johnson," Rat greeted the old man.

"What are you children doing outdoors when it is raining like this?"

"We running away," Duute spoke up.

Rat and Duute were inseparable. Since the time when Rat was three and she carried Duute on her hip when he was a newborn to show him to her cousins, he was her baby. She took him everywhere that she went.

"What you running away for?"

"Momma going to whop us," Duute declared.

"Well sit down here and wait for the rain to stop. Your momma must be worried about you."

Mister Johnson was one of the last remaining former slaves alive. He was an old man now, but he was born on the plantation. He had lived the experience of slavery and freedom. He told many stories of that time.

"Every Sunday, they gave us a biscuit filled with sugar."

The children listen to every word the Mister Johnson spoke. Rat enjoyed listening to the old people talk, and so did Duute.

"Was it good?" Rat asked.

"It was all we had."

"Did you come from Africa?" Rat knew about Africa because she went to school.

"What is Africa?" asked Duute.

"No, I didn't come from Africa."

"My teacher said we came from Africa."

"Well, some folks come from Africa and some don't. Folks from around these parts don't come from Africa. At least not like they are teaching in school."

"Well, where we come from then?"

"Where we come from? Right here," Mister Johnson answered the little one.

"They say we Africans?"

"Africans?" wondered Duute.

"No such thing. This ain't Africa and we ain't Africans. At least that's what my daddy told me."

"Well what are we then?" Rat had to know.

Mister Johnson sat back in his chair for a minute or two as if he were recollecting a long forgotten memory. He sat thinking about what he was going to say. He was trying to remember it like his daddy had told him.

"Long time ago these folk that's here now wasn't here. They come from Europe. We were here before them."

"You mean we are Indians. Momma says we Saponi and Maherrin."

"What's that?" asked little Duute.

"Now maybe, but I ain't talking about Indians neither. I am talking about the original man who was here first."

The children eyes grew wider as Mister Johnson started to tell the story to them. They knew that whatever he was going to tell them they wanted to hear it. That was why they like to listen to old people talk, because they had all kinds of stories to tell.

"What is original man?" Rat asked.

"Long time ago there wasn't Indians here neither," Mister Johnson said.

"It was empty land," Rat guessed.

"No. Used to be another people here. Used to be another country. Different people. Everything was different," Mister Johnson began.

"What people was that, Mister Johnson?"

"Our people didn't always live here in Virginia. We used to live in another place. They had to move here because of the war."

"What war? The Civil War?"

"No, not the Civil War. 'The Greatest War'. First I am going to tell you the whole story, because 'The Greatest War' is the end." Mister Johnson opened his eyes wide, then closed them tightly trying to picture in his mind what he wanted to convey.

"Long, long time ago this here place we call America used be filled with all kinds of folks like it is now. There were visitors coming here from all over the world. I'm talking about long before the British, French, Portuguese, and Spanish. First, there was some folks come from Africa because that's where all original folks come from.

These African folks came and built a new nation. Well, at least they brought the African civilization here with them. They built everything here that they built in Africa. They built pyramids, cities, roads, and canals. These Africans was from the same Africans that built Egypt and Babylon.

They traveled in ships all over the world. They were seamen and they knew the seas in the most intimate way. Back then it wasn't any Atlantic ocean. It was the Ethiopian ocean. This land was always rich so people from all over the world wanted her goods in trade. Oh, yea, this land was a wonderful place back then. And everybody was free."

*****

"Captain, we are in view of Washitaw harbor," the first mate reported to the captain of the Olmec vessel.

"It's good to be home again. Prepare to make port and unload the cargo," said Tidasi. He had been out to sea most of his life. This was to be his last expedition. Now he would move onto the land to complete the fullness of life. He was of the latest of the Olmec explorers from Aztalan. He would be happy to see Nosh, Mona,

Tallulah, Ayasha, and Elan after such an extended time. He was part of the merchant fleet that had circumnavigated the world.

Tidasi had been born in Aztalan at Cahokia. He had taken to the river and the sea at an early age as all the men of his family had done for generations. As a young waterman he had charted all the rivers within the Mississippi system. This was a duty of all Aztalan youth who wanted to become seamen. Tidasi had trained at La Venta, the traditional home of Olmec seamanship.

"Captain, the seas will miss you. We will all miss you," the first mate added.

Washitaw harbor was a deep water harbor at the mouth of the Mississippi River. The Gulf of Anahuac saw constant movement of merchant vessels to Tabasco and onward.

It had been a long voyage. The men were happy to return home from their merchant trip to Cush. Xi could not have been a more welcomed sight. The Xi province was the main port of call within the domain of Anahuac. "The people" of Xi were considered the best seamen in the world. They had learned to ride the Gulf Stream so efficiently that they could make the trip from Anahuac to Cush and back in weeks instead of months.

The Mississippi was second only to the Nile in age as the oldest river in the world. Others types of ships would continue upriver passing the many cities that stood within sight of the banks of the Mississippi. The jewel of the Mississippi was Cahokia.

Others on the ship would continue their voyage across to the peninsula and onto Teotihuacan, The City of Tehuti, the southern capital of Anahuac, and others would go even further. Kemanahuac comprised both of the great continents of the Western Hemisphere. It was Anahuac that was the Promised Land. The Cushite civilization under Osiris had been broken up and "the people" took hope in the promise of this land.

The Cushite civilization of the west was indeed as splendid as that in Africa and Asia including Egypt, Babylon, India, and China. The Cushite civilization was a world encompassing civilization. Aztalan, located within the Mississippi River Valley, was the greatest source of copper and other minerals in the world. It was the source of all the rich copper that used during the Copper and Bronze Ages.

"We are a prosperous and peaceful nation. Our navy is the best trained in the world. Our civilization will stand for thousands of years. Our way of life is made to carry on. We welcome visitors from all over the world. Our brothers from Egypt, Phut, and Canaan are here living and trading with us, as is Carthage, and others. We all belong to the seas. How could there be a better time to live in? This is where you belong, Tidasi," the amir told Tidasi attempting to convince him to stay, "You belong to the sea and it to you."

It was a fact that Anahuac was an open and accepting country. There was diversity everywhere including in religions. Judaism, Christianity, Islam had come with the Egyptians and others. It also appeared that the Europeans had made their appearance at some time. "The people" of Anahuac, ancient America, had known visitors from all over the world. It appeared that the last to come were the last to know about the land of promise. It was those who had claimed to discover America who were the ones now waking up.

"I will miss the sea, but my family needs me. It is my time to return to the land," Tidasi said. "The sea has been my home for so long that I also love it. Is it like leaving an old friend. So I won't say good-bye, but until we meet again."

"Of course, you are correct. Our families must come first. Family is the basis of our civilization," the amir returned.

"Thank you, sir. It was an honor to serve with you."

"Thank you, Tidasi."

The Olmec were the gate keepers of the civilization of the west which was identical to the civilization to the east, Cush. They had come to this land so long ago at the beginning of civilization there were considered two easts and two wests. They were still one people. They were all still Cushites and "the people" of Cush. It was they who had their roots in the building of the Egyptian African Civilization and they had done the same thing in Anahuac. Egypt and Anahuac had a common origin and that was Cush.

Cahokia was a fabulous city that was the image of excellence like all the other previous attempts by the Cushites to build civilization. It was different only in design but not in sophistication. Cahokia was a fabulous city that was a marvel of genius. The Olmec came to realize that the practicality of engineering with locally produced renewable materials was how to harmonize with continuity. To prove that this could be done they built pyramids as mighty as the ones of Egypt and China.

It was the great river system which gave glory to the region. It was here that the Missouri and Illinois rivers met and joined with the Mississippi to produce some of the most alluvial land in the world. The confluence of the Mississippi and Ohio met like the white and blue branches of Africa's Nile at a place called Cairo in Illinois. The high quality of the soil was produced in the same way that it was in Egypt, through annual flooding.

There existed a vast network of waterways based on the rivers and canals that would rival any transportation system at any time. The knowledge that the Cushites had experienced with the engineering of the Nile lent itself fully to the extraordinary design of the ancient American waterway system.

The infrastructure was kept viable by the complex system of canals which crisscrossed the landscape. These canals were long and deep enough for two barges to pass simultaneously in opposite directions. The canals allowed for the transportation of goods throughout Anahuac. "The people" of Anahuac also built canals which were the length and breadth of rivers. In fact, the large canals would later be mistaken for rivers. By using local resources and working in harmony with nature the founders of the Ancient American Civilization gave inspiration to ingenuity.

"Cahokia," shouted the mate to the passengers who wanted to disembark.

Long before the riverboat came in view of Cahokia the signs of an urban center could be seen. From the banks of the shore tree-lined avenues and boulevards led to the city. "The people" enjoyed the gift of the Mississippi as a source of commerce and recreation. As Tidasi's boat continued there came into view a magnificent sight. From the Mississippi, the Great Pyramid of Cahokia could be seen towering into the air in all its splendor. It was the largest structure by volume on the continent. The elegance of Cahokia lay in its urban planning. This city like all the Cushites cities in the world was an outstanding feat of civil engineering and urban design. This structure was the epitome of the dreams of "the people". The Great Pyramid was more than a megalithic monument. It was a power generating machine that had come to identify the genius that were the Cushites. In Egypt, Anahuac, and elsewhere the pyramid was the symbol of the Cushite civilization and its extent.

"Cahokia," Tidasi repeated to himself. Even he stood in awe of the city in which he was born. Cahokia was a metropolitan area of about one hundred thousand and was larger than both Paris and London combined at the time. Cahokia was even more important because it was also the spiritual capital of the north as well. The city's prestige lay in its ties to the Cushite Empire of which it was a part. The Cushite Empire encircled the world with no less than forty five nations. The Dominion of Anahuac was the northwest of the Cushite domain.

"Tidasi!" Tallulah shouted from the peer as her husband came to shore on one of the many barges that waited for the boats that moved up or down the river daily. The Mississippi was the busiest highway in the world. Tidasi had missed his family and only heard news of them when he received the occasional letter during port calls. He missed his children, Ayasha and Elan, more than anything. Seeing Tallulah and the children again made him forget forever about returning to the sea.

"My love", Tidasi said as he embraced his wife, picked up his children, and held them all close.

The entire family was there waiting to receive him. There were hugs and kisses from everyone. There were all those whom he had not seen for a long time. There were also the new additions through marriage and births who welcomed him. This was the way that all the returning voyagers were received by their families.

They made it to the longhouse of the family. The longhouse was the communal home where sometimes four generations of family would live together. Tidasi could not image any other way of life.

When he entered the longhouse he saw the old man, Nosh and his mother, Mona. Nosh, his father, was the center of life in his life. His father was the center of his family. Nosh had taken to and returned from the seas long ago. He was respected for his life's work.

"Father," Tidasi fell to his knees in prostration to his father. "Mother,"

Whispers of a Man 11

he said turning to kiss the hand of his mother.

"I am happy that you have returned. The young need you. They need the lessons from your adventures. We all need the wisdom that you have gained added to our own as mine was added," said Nosh.

"Tidasi," one of the young men called.

"Enapay. You have grown so much. And is that Cheveyo, and Kitchi?" These were Tidasi's brothers who were waiting their turns to go on adventures around the world.

Tallulah stood proudly at the side of her husband. He had returned a true man of Cahokia. He had gone on many journeys and had many stories to tell. Their son Elan listened to his grandfather, father, and uncles each take the floor telling and retelling the adventures of their lives. Here there was something in being a storyteller.

Story's were a part of the way of life. These stories were based on the life of a man. In this way the family would know the men of the family. Each man wanted to tell the stories of his adventures to his family. So each wanted to go out into the world to find his story.

"What have you seen, Tidasi?" Nosh, the chief of the longhouse asked his son.

"I have seen the two easts and the two wests. I have the crossed the Ethiopian ocean and sailed the Nile. I have seen what our people have left behind as evidence of their existence for thousands of years. There are no secrets."

"What were the accomplishments of our ancestors?" asked Heluska, the friend of Tidasi who had also seen the seas and the adventures of the world.

"Heluska," Tidasi said, as he embraced his lifelong friend who he loved like a brother. "I saw the work of Tehuti in Africa was as marvelous as his work here. He was the world's master builder. His work in Saqqara and Giza do not rival but compliment his mastery in Teotihuacan, Cholula, and Cahokia."

"What does that mean, father?" asked Elan, the son of Tidasi.

"It means that our family lives everywhere on this world. We are one nation and one people."

"My son, you have seen and learned much," said Nosh admiring his son's adventures. "You are correct in your observation of our enlighten teacher, Tehuti. We go to sea and return with stories of adventure to keep vigor in the lives and spirits of "the people". Let us never forget those who traveled this way before us. Let us never forget the great Law of the One."

Tehuti was the same Djehuti of Egypt. He was the master architect, inventor of writing, writer of the three-hundred sixty books concerning all matters, and the designer of the three-hundred sixty five day calendar who was revered by all. During the time of Zep Tepi the Cushites were in possession of the technology from the first world. It was Osiris who was the pharaoh to the entire world. And it was Osiris who was the initial object of sun worship. In the west Osiris was more than revered.

"We travel the world to see what has become of those who have gone before us so we may always remember why the Olmec exist," Nosh continued.

It was the worship of Osiris as the sun god that proved to be the root cause of the ultimate downfall of the Olmec. There arose within the Olmec a faction of those who wanted to continue the worship of Baal in opposition to the following of the Law of the One. This faction became known as the Maya. It was the war with the Maya that prove to be the destruction of the Cushite Olmec civilization. In defeating the Maya the Olmec themselves were almost completely destroyed as well. The entire civilization was sacrificed so sun worship would not consume the whole of Kemanahuac. The last baston of the weakened civilization remained in Aztalan and Cahokia.

"It was the Olmec who brought civilization to this land. And even they could not prevent disease from spreading among "the people". The Maya were their children," said Nosh.

The Olmec had no choice other than to remove the Maya from existence in Kemanahuac. The Maya were an off shoot and the progeny of the Olmec who had determined to revive and resurrect Osiris. While the Olmec were the last protectors of the Law of the One the civil war that rage between the Olmec-Maya family marked the end of Zep Tepi in the west.

The Maya were the once enlightened who chose darkness instead of light and became corrupted. They then began to see themselves as different from the Olmec, who continued to embrace the original way. The Maya began to dominate those weaker than themselves. Once they began to dominate others balance was lost.

The Maya were finally vanquish and exiled from the land in ships. They never returned. They were an advance people of Olmec and Cushites descent who had forgotten the law. They became extremist and fanatical about the existential relationship between man, science, and the environment.

However, this civil war had left civilization with no more taste for warfare and the tools of warfare began rust and fade into dust.

"We must remember the struggle of our ancestors to defend this land from those who would follow darkness," spoke Nosh. "The people" began to stir with a commotion.

"Hiamovi," someone said.

It was the governmental ruler who was about to speak to "the people". Hiamovi was from among them and had been elected Ku Tu upon his return from the sea and his excursions to the wilderness of the east. He was loved by "the people" and often told stories of the evidences that he had found of those who had gone before. Under Hiamovi there was no war and peace reigned.

"Dohiyi, peace," Hiamovi opened in speaking to "the people" of Cahokia. "We live in times of prosperity. Our children are well feed and our elderly are healthy. We must never forget the One who gives us life and abundance. All of you who have seen other lands know that this land is a sacred land. Although we are friends to all men it may not be true that all men will return our friendship.

Our maze grows the tallest and our runners are the fastest. Our men are tall and the strong. Our women are beautiful and strong. Our people are satisfied because they have enough and no one is in need. It is because of the relationship that we maintain with this land and the relationship that this land maintains with us that we prosper. We are of this land and this land is of us.

When you speak to the Great One who has made all things do not forget that we must give in peace something of what we have been given. Give a smile to your neighbor if he needs nothing else. Possess not the land or anything or anyone else. Give peace to all things and we shall have peace always."

Hiamovi looked upon the thousands of people who had gathered to hear his words. He was speaking to them about complacency. "The people" were tuned and enjoyed listening to wisdom.

"The peace that we enjoy today is not a peace as opposed to war because there is no war," he said. "We have enjoyed peace for many generations because we have not known war."

Because "the people" were not warlike they were able acclimate themselves to fuller pursuits. "The people" of Cahokia were able to do marvelous things. They were able to harness the power of the river system as a source of energy. In the land of the Mississippi River system there was abundance. The buffalo and deer herds numbered into the millions. The harvest and crop yields made Aztalan the breadbasket of the world.

"The people" of Aztalan were also master metallurgists because of their extensive experience with copper and other metals. They had mastered a particular type of battery. They knew how to make glass and excite gases trapped inside to produce light. Electricity was well known throughout the ancient world including Anahuac. "The people" of Cahokia were able to draw energy from both the river and the land.

"The people" continued to listen to Hiamovi, "Live your dreams. Speak not of letting the single instances of life slip away."

That was also one of the important reasons why the youth were so eager to take to the seas. Each of them had zest for life and zeal to grasp the moment. They grew to possess the spirit of freedom. They were all brave.

"The people" of Aztalan and Cahokia in particular were extremely tall. They were of bronze colored skin and wore their hair in locks. They were of a mild manner and a gentle disposition. Violent dispute was something that they did not exist in their mind-sets. The men were however very powerful. Each of them was taught to grapple starting at the age of five years. Grappling was one of the mainstays of life for the boys and girls of Aztalan. It was commonly agreed that the best grapplers in Anahuac were from Cahokia.

"The people" were not simply a peaceful people but a people without pride. Because the land was prosperous "the people" were prosperous. There was no poverty and the ownership of land was not necessary. It was understood that when a people were living together in harmony with nature there could be no poverty, and greed was not known because all "the people" had abundance.

"We are among the richest nations on Earth. We do not know poverty and laziness. Each of you is a producer and productive. We do not know inequality and we do not know slavery. When we travel the lands of the world we see the faults of mankind. We see the bickering, slavery, and wars," the Ku Tu continued. "That is why Carthage and others have come to us seeking knowledge and trade."

It was this great estate that lay between the Rocky and Allegheny mountains where the most harmonious civilization existed. It was simply rich without any being poor. Without being poor meant the absence of poverty. Aztalan was the Promised Land.

The Cushite Empire had become weaken all over the world because of the civil war with the Maya and their allies. Still the Cushites stood for enlightenment and freedom. In the west the Cushites had lost the taste for war and were evolving into highest state of man.

In the Western Hemisphere the Cushites were also more inaccessible to the barbarians from the north. Civilization was under threat from the Northern Horde. "The people" of Anahuac had not bothered to build walls such as the Great Wall, the Gorgan Wall, and the Caucasian Wall to keep the barbarians out. The northern lands were frozen solid and impassable.

"Long ago our ancestors followed Tehuti's teachings and moved to Anahuac. Tehuti's teachings gives us knowledge and light while Egypt, Babylon, and India are threatened by the barbarians from the north. We are the light of the world keeping darkness at bay," Hiamovi said.

The center of civilization had been relocated to Kemanahuac, the combined North and South America. In moving the center of civilization from Africa/Amexum to America/Anahuac the Cushites made a definitive testimony with Ancient American civilization.

It was Teotihuacan, with its magnificent pyramids, that was the restoration of the preflood civilization of Zep Tepi. As Zep Tepi had revived civilization after the flood in Africa and Asia it did the same thing in the Anahuac. Teotihuacan was not the oldest city in Anahuac. That honor went to Tenochtitlan which had stood since it had been dedicated by Cain, the son of Adam to his son Enoch. The history of Anahuac went back to the beginning of man's reign on Earth.

"Our civilization has encircled the world since our forefathers came from the Mountains of the Moon at the source of the Nile in Africa. They gave the gift of civilization. We are the last remaining holders of the custodianship of that civilization. It is Anahuac which is the continued hope of civilization."

Following the Great Flood it had been the descendants of Noah who had rebuilt civilization worldwide. It was the Cushite Olmec who first arrived from the west of Africa. Following sometime thereafter were the Shang of China who were also Cushites. At that time all people of the Earth were one people, "the people". They were the descendants of Noah and his sons.

Building upon the foundation that the Olmec lay the Olmec and the Shang built the complete society of the Kemanahuac, the Americas. Then through a doctrine of diversity and inclusion the Cushite civilization in the west flourished to greatness. It was then that the ancient American civilization reached its zenith. Man had come full circle and had learned to harmonize with himself, with nature, and with the nature of existence. This was why man existed at that time.

"We know that we are all brothers. The buffalo and the deer are our brothers. The river and the sky are also our brothers. This is the secret that we carry. We carry the secret of spirit within us. We are not spiritual, but we are spirit. And there is a difference. Being spiritual is to spirit as mankind is to man. They are both lesser in comparison to the greater," said Hiamovi. "We are speaking about soul. Soul is what connects and binds us with everything. That is why your brothers and sisters don't fear you. That is why the animals don't fear you. There is no need because we all got soul."

Tidasi listened to Hiamovi speak his mighty words. He could feel the reverberation of every syllable. All of "the people" could feel the spirit in the words that Hiamovi spoke. They all knew that Aztalan was a special place. They knew that they were the last keepers of the knowledge which was becoming lost in Egypt, India, China, and Babylon. They knew that this knowledge of wisdom and spirit must not be lost in Anahuac.

"Hiamovi speaks the truth," said Nosh back at the longhouse, "He and I traveled and saw the world together. We have taken the pledge of brotherhood from childhood."

"Why did you not become Ku Tu?" asked Ayasha.

"I voted for him," answered Nosh. "And we could not have a better Ku Tu. For us there is no difference between the stars and the Earth. To look into the night sky is to look into one's own home. I can see that Hiamovi cares for me more than I care for myself. To have someone who watches over you so that you have no worries is worth everything. That is a true friend."

The experience of the Cushites was a lesson in self-realization. It was the realization that man was an infinite and capable of the divine. Man also knew that as there was harmony there would be disharmony. He studied the law of opposites. With disharmony came the lowering of the gaze to a level below the horizon. Once the flint of chaos was introduced into man the west began to deteriorate as rapidly as the rest of the world. Man was attempting keep knowledge of self and maintain his base.

The remnants of the followers of the One attempted to maintain balance and harmony. Cahokia was the great extent of the Cushite civilization. And it was Hiamovi, Nosh, and the others who kept the spirit alive. The Olmec legacy was worth recounting over and over. Weakened was the glory of Teotihuacan and long past its height was Tenochtitlan. The concentration of civilization rested in Aztalan with its capital at Cahokia. It was here that the Cushite civilization made its last stand. Aztalan became renowned for its maintenance of that civilization.

"You see, Tidasi, everyone is here to welcome you home. Our Ku Tu, who is brother to your father, has gathered all "the people" in the advent of you homecoming," said Heluska.

"The people" then all came to Tidasi welcoming and kissing him again. It was when Hiamovi, himself, came to embrace Tidasi that the emotion overwhelmed him from within. Hiamovi had many daughters, but no sons, and he loved Tidasi as his own.

"Tidasi, 'the people' have always awaited the return of our seamen. Your return is a very special one. There are stirring in the air and a bitter wind is approaching. We will need you and all the young men who have knowledge soon."

"Why Hiamovi?" asked Tidasi.

"We are the last of our kind. Within the world there are but small remembrances of our origins. Most of the knowledge is now fragmented and lost. These are the last proofs of the past," said Hiamovi. Hiamovi then had two golden plates that had been made by Tehuti himself brought forward.

"These golden plates contain the history of our people. They must be protected and kept safe. We are the bearers of this sacred knowledge."

Tidasi examined the golden plates carefully. He fully reflected on the hieratic writing with which they were scripted. He could read the writing. It was written in Cushite. This was the same hieratic and the common script used worldwide.

"These plates must never be lost," said Hiamovi. "I am entrusting them to your care for protection".

Nosh looked proudly at his son as the Ku Tu gave him the honor of protecting the golden plates. This was the greatest honor that the family of Nosh could have bestowed upon them. His son had been chosen above all others.

Chapter 2

Enapay, Cheveyo, and Kitchi waited in the thicket on horseback watching a herd of giant buffalo that drink from a stream. Then the trio made their move by charging all out in a parallel tract to the fleeing buffalo. Kitchi galloped his horse behind the herd pushing them constantly. Cheveyo had crossed the stream and was riding parallel on the other side. The mighty herd moved with the sound of thunder. The three brothers of Tidasi did not relent. This was the beginning of a great dance taking place.

Tidasi and Heluska watched from a high hill as Kitchi's horse ran it seemed on the water. Heluska made his move down the hill in a dash straight into the heart of the herd. This tactic immediately confused the oncoming buffalo. They then split into two columns going to the right and the left. The men let the column on the left escape.

They managed to cull a single giant buffalo bull from the herd. The animal rose up in self-defense. The buffalo raise its mighty horns in a display of defiance. Tidasi took a long aim with his lance and atlatl. The atlatl was a throwing stick which gave the lance greater distance and striking power. He hurled the lance at the mighty beast. The lance pierced the thick hide of the great animal. The angry animal now took his own aim moving forward toward Tidasi with a vengeance.

Heluska, who was still pursuing the buffalo from the blind side, took aim with his lance. He drew back strongly and let go. His lance pierced the great buffalo through its side. The buffalo was now very angry and continued to bear down on Tidasi. Heluska was still charging the blind side of the buffalo, and with a powerful leap he mounted the animal.

Heluska held strongly onto the mane of the buffalo while plunging his copper knife into its throat. The powerful buffalo became even more powerful and angry with the assault. He reared and bucked mightily until Heluska was sent flying from his mount. The others had dismounted their horses and charged selflessly at the injured and dangerous giant buffalo to distract him. The buffalo grew still angrier and ignored the distractions.

It seemed that the animal was breathing fire as he prepared to make his charge at the fallen Heluska. Tidasi then made a powerful leap onto the back of the buffalo and plunge his long knife into its throat as Heluska had done. He cut long and deep into the animal. Tidasi held on to the buffalo and would not let go. His entire arm has disappeared in the throat of the beast. The head of the animal was as large as a boulder.

The buffalo drop to its front knees and bucked again and again. Tidasi would not let go. He maintained his mount. The buffalo though mortally injured was moved by its anger. Once again the buffalo took its aim. It was determined to take one of them with him. This time it was Enapay who caught its sight.

The buffalo made a powerful leap into the air toward Enapay. With copper tipped lance in hand Enapay knelt before the animal extending to meet the buffalo's leap. Into the heart of the great beast did Enapay's lance pierce. The giant buffalo dropped to the ground and did not move again. Tidasi was still on its back with his arm deep in the throat of the beast.

This struggle had ended when the mighty giant buffalo was fallen lifeless. Tidasi dismounted the buffalo to check on Enapay. He had survived the leap of the buffalo unharmed, and Heluska, who had taken hard fall, stood strongly unharmed as well.

Cheveyo and Kitchi stood proudly over the animal. Then the five said a prayer for the life of the great buffalo and a prayer for their own lives which had not been lost. It was in all sincerity that they gave thanks. They gave thanks to the One who had given this mighty beast the life that it had fought so hard to keep.

It was law and not religion that was the foundation of life of "the

Whispers of a Man

people". They had come to see the closeness of all things through the equanimity of all under the law. The law made the religion the practice of spirit. Though the buffalo had fallen it was not dead. It would live through the food it provided. It would carry on in the warmth that its coat would provide in winter. The meat of the buffalo would feed hundreds. Nothing would be wasted, and nothing would be thrown away. In fact, every single part of the animal was used for something.

It was the law that gave "the people" of Cahokia their connection with eternity. The law required that they be virtuous. They did not build places of worship. All under heaven was a place of worship and every act an act of devotion. Law and religion were not dialectically opposed, because the law was all encompassing and the law of the One was the basis of the law.

They connected with the past and they connected with the land. By this time there had come to the land many religions. "The people" had realized that it was not religion which would be their motivation but a connection with all things. They had come to realize that it was the great and mighty buffalo which had come to teach them how to live. The religion of "the people" was peace, harmony, and devotion.

Nosh and Hiamovi stood in the distance watching as the hunt had taken place. Tallulah, Ayasha, and Elan were also witness to the tradition of the hunt. They understood the importance of giving thanks before the first drop of blood had touched the earth. Soon the women and men from Cahokia were taking part in the butcher of the buffalo. All would share in this reward. This buffalo belonged to them all.

Today would be the beginning Festival of Harvest. There was abundance and the spirit of the One moved among "the people". The most of "the people" of Cahokia would take part in the games. Chunkey was a game that all of "the people" enjoyed. It was played by rolling a ball across a yard, and the men would show their skill by throwing a lance in attempt to pierce the moving target. This was the source of the skill with the lance. "The people" from all over Aztalan would come to participate in the event. The event was designed to bring "the people" together. Chunkey yards literally dotted the landscape of the Cahokia.

"I am next," said Kitchi.

"So you think you are ready little brother," said Enapay playfully.

"Let us see what you have," added Cheveyo.

The family all stood watching the brothers challenge one another in Chunky. Kitchi took careful aim with his lance and let go. He struck the Chunky ball dead in the center. The cheers went up from the family, and everyone laughed.

"Way to go Kitchi," said Tidasi. "That was excellent."

The rest took their turns not to be out done by Kitchi. He was the youngest of the sons of Nosh. Now he had reached sixteen years of age. He could now take his place alongside of the men.

"Heluska is still the best I think," said Cheveyo.

Tidasi took up his lance and fired through the center of the ball. He was expert in all the traditional ways of "the people". He was expected to be the one of best. Heluska then took up three lance and fired them in secession through the centers of three balls. The crowd cheered loudly.

"You are still the best," said Tidasi to Heluska. Tidasi lived for the moment when he could compete against his family and friends in fun. "The people" got to enjoy the company of others in this way. The game kept going on.

"The people" also played the ancient and original form of the game of lacrosse. Lacrosse was played in the large sports field adjacent to the Great Pyramid of Cahokia. The rules of the games were few. "The people" did not like to disrupt the continuity and spontaneity of the game. This game was played as the symbolic representation of war. The purpose of this game and all sports were to act as a catharsis and to purge "the people" of any ignoble impulses. It was played with hundreds of players participating in a single game. It was after this game that the feast would take place.

In preparation for feasting the women would prepare food for days. The staples of the feast were wild rice, corn, kneel down bread, turkey, buffalo stew, deer, fish, squash, pumpkin, apples, blueberry pudding, cakes, and teas. There were all kinds of deserts and sweets were served as well.

"It's so good to have him back," said Tallulah. She like all women of Cahokia were the maintainers of the family while the husbands went to the seas. The women were unique because they were the experts in commerce and fiscal planning. The main role of the women of Cahokia were as managers of the infrustructure of the society. At every level and walk of life women were integral to economic security. "The people" did not know chauvinism.

"This is the new coat that I made for Tidasi," Tallulah said.

"It's beautiful," said Mona, Tidasi's mother.

The women took great pride in the creation of beautiful things. They especially took creating themselves in the image of beauty with care. Tallulah's skin was the color of honey kissed by the sun. Her beauty radiated from the depth within. She was a natural beauty made perfect without need for improvement or embellishment. This was not just true of Tallulah but was also true of all of "the people". They were the beautiful people.

"You need to be alone with your husband," said Mona. "I know when Nosh returned from the sea we disappeared for two weeks."

They laughed, while Tallulah prepared a very special and personal meal for her husband. They had married when Tidasi was eighteen. They had found each other in love. Each had freely accepted the responsibility of having entered into marriage with the other. The only contract that was needed was that which bound them to the sacred law of marriage. In this way they found completeness in marriage to one another.

The harvest was a show of devotion to the One. It was evidence of the favor that was bestowed upon "the people". Even eating was an act of devotion. Every activity that "the people" undertook was done in the showing of grace and appreciation for what had been received.

Long into the night "the people" were treated to acrobats and circus tricks perform by talented entertainers. Delegates from all over Anahuac were arriving at this time. The lights of Cahokia would burn long this night. The lighted avenues crisscrossed. Every home had a light burning in the front of it.

The Mississippi became full of boats and barges with people from up and down the river coming to join in the celebration. The men would gather to tell stories of adventures of the hunt. They would talk of the brave buffalo that would rise to the challenge of the hunt and its attempt to become the hunter.

Some of the men wore the scars of the hunt. In some cases the buffalo would win the contest and one of the men of "the people" would go down. This was the price of the high honor of participation in the hunt. The buffalo was given an equal chance to be successful. In fact the buffalo did not have to be given anything. The buffalo was the largest and most powerful animal on the continent since the demise of the mastodon.

The next day the males and the girls of Cahokia would gather to grapple. The contestants were grouped based upon age. All of "the people" loved grappling. Of all the sports it was the most popular. Girls would participate up until they married usually at the of sixteen. Physical fitness was not thought of deliberately as a way of life. It was simply a way to maintain good health and strong bodies. And it was a natural thing that "the people" had always done.

"Okay honey it's your turn," Tallulah said to Ayasha. Ayasha was always grappling with the boys all the time and was very good.

"Come Dyani," the mother of Ayasha's opponent encouraged her own daughter.

The two little girls moved like kittens with no hesitation. They were well trained at this young age. Both had the tenacity and intensity to win. The match ended when Ayasha caught Dyani in an arm lock forcing a submission. Neither girl was injured and they both enjoyed the match. Soon they forget about grappling went off to play with butterflies.

The grappling matches between men brought the largest crowds. The rules were simple, grapple until a submission. There were no time limits. The matches would go on sometimes for hours. The style was similar to the Jiu-jitsu of Brazil with the exception of adding extremely painful leg locking techniques. The technique which was applied to grappling most often was the pressure point attack and not just a hyper-extension of joint. Chokes were also applied. In grappling there was the application of strength through superior conditioning, courage through bravery, and technique through practice. Yet, truth in sportsmanship was the greatest virtue. The grapplers loved to grapple and they loved other grapplers.

All the men who were able were expected to participate in the tournament. Tidasi and Heluska stood in the center of the grappling circle. They were both experts in the art since childhood. They had grappled with each other hundreds of times.

"Are you ready my brother?" asked an amused Heluska. "You have been away for some time."

A huge crowd gathered to watch the match. Hiamovi and Nosh also were in attendance. The two men stood before one another with faces and bodies painted in traditional way. The command to begin was given. With one hand held high and the other held low they two stalked each other in the center of the circle. Heluska open with a bear hug body lock. Tidasi countered the technique by dropping his hips.

Tidasi laughed, "You are right I may be a little rusty." Then Tidasi launched Heluska with a high arcing throw. "Not that rusty."

The crowd stood in amazement as the two best friends played the game of catch as catch can. Heluska was not so easily fooled and landed on his feet. He then countered by rebounding on to his hands, and then in a back flip placing himself behind Tidasi.

"Do you remember this one my brother," said Heluska still laughing. Heluska in an amazingly athletic move continued countering by applying a flying arm lock.

"Yes, I remember." Tidasi somersaulted the assault and caught Heluska in his double leg knee lock. Heluska writhe in pain as Tidasi applied pressure to the lock. Heluska lay on his back while Tidasi lay opposite continuing to apply pressure to his knee. Unable to tolerate the pain further Heluska signaled in order to signify resignation.

The two laughed like little boys. They played the game of catch as catch can at it highest level. The legs of the two had to be untangled by others. Once this double leg knee lock was applied it was very difficult to extricate oneself without breaking the leg of the opponent.

The two friends embraced arms and returned to sit. Tidasi was very grateful that Heluska was there to give him the opportunity to raise his spirit and to experience the rush of life. He was thankful to his friend for making his heartbeat faster and his breath harder.

Heluska was loved by "the people" of Cahokia. He and his wife Aiyana were expecting their third child soon. They lived in the longhouse of his family near the longhouse of Nosh. He and Tidasi had been friends since they had charted the branches of the Mississippi together so long ago. Since that time they had both gone out to sea and now returned. Friends they would always be.

The two friends laughed at the feigned intensity of their battle. They laughed as children would laugh. They knew that to grapple was just another way for two friends express friendship. Each was an expert so their competition could be relentless. It was the relentlessness of the action that gave "the people" cause to marvel. The two waged battle in the spirit of the jaguar.

On this night the men and women who were of age would sit before the council chamber which was adjacent to the Great Pyramid. It was always at this time of year after the festival of the harvest that the elected government of Anahuac would convene to discuss the business of "the people". The location rotated each year and this the convention was held in Cahokia. Hiamovi would preside over the convention.

Also present was Peto, Eagles Rib, from "the people" of the Missouri. There was Tawanah, Mountain of Rocks, who represented the southwest. Oshkosh was also there to represent "the people" of the north Aztalan. The Cushite descendants from all over Anahuac convened at Cahokia including Osceola, Mickenpah, and Tawanaquenah from their respective lands. And Panowau represented the Mengwe.

"We are 'the people'," said Hiamovi. "This statement is more than a mere expression of words. This is a statement of fact and conviction. This is an affirmation of who we are. We are tried and tested by time and trial. 'The people' have come this long way since the beginning with the Annu, our ancestors. This chain is unbroken."

The laws were few and based on the right of "the people" to liberty. It was without infringement on the rights of man, animals, and Earth that harmony and peace did prevailed. The laws that had been developed were old laws that were founded in the settling of disputes without bringing harm or dishonor to another.

"Each year 'the people' gathered to reaffirm our existence and reconsider our relations under the law. It is the simplicity and purity of the law which makes our civilization beautiful. It is the openness of our chamber that gives precedence to our government. All the 'the people' bear witness to the proceedings inside these chambers. Our law forbids closed-door meetings."

The fundamental law of the land was "without prejudice". No rights of any individual could be suspended at any time. This further meant that though an individual may be unaware of the law his ignorance could not be used against him. This was to be interpreted so no one could be represented by any entity other than himself. There could be no proxy in litigation. Therefore in all matters did the individual maintain his rights.

Each time a new law was considered it was done as an amendment to an existing law. In this way "the people" were not over burden with too many laws. All laws were recorded in stone and all laws were reconciled to the law that was recorded in the golden plates by Tehuti. The law was simple. The basic issue pertaining to the implementation of new laws was whether there was deviation from the law that had been given to "the people" by the One, as recorded by Tehuti.

Very rarely could there by a new law proclaimed. If a new law were to be initiated then a referendum had to be placed before "the people" and the entire community would vote on the issue. And if that referendum passed then that law was also writing in stone. All votes counted equally. There were never any political parties of any kind.

Overstanding the law was principle. The law was the guiding virtue by which all men were to be a standard bearer. It was in the virtue of the Law of the One that "the people" found solace. The principle of virtue gave to "the people" the basis of civilization. It was in this way that everyone maintained the element and root of civilization within themselves. It was law that was maintained as foundation of civilization.

The council sat speaking far into the night about the law as it had been originally recorded by Tehuti. He had left them with the storehouse of knowledge with which to maintain man as a conscious entity.

"The purpose of the law is act as the guidance in cases of dispute. This law is never meant to oppress anyone," said Hiamovi to the delegates. "It has been very rarely that a new law has been added. Therefore, "the people" know the law."

All the delegates knew the body of the law of the land. This was the law that was common to all. They all sat quietly and reverently listening to Hiamovi recited the law.

"We must never kill any human being except in the defense of our own lives.

Never know any woman besides our own,

Never take something that belongs to another,

Never lie,

Do not drink alcohol,

Do not be avaricious,

Give generously and with joy,

And Share our subsistence with those who are in need of it," said Hiamovi reciting the law.

These were the laws of the land that had not been added to nor taken away from since Tehuti had recorded them. It was with this basis that "the people" live their lives in harmony with all and they were not over burdened by the law.

As the great fire of the council was finishing its burn and before the sun came up. All of "the people" of Cahokia turn to the east to pray. It was Hiawatha who would lead them in paying homage to the One.

"We give praise and thanks to the One who has created all things from nothing. From a thought he has willed all things into being. It is the Great Spirit that is the One in All who has guided us with our honored teacher, and who also teaches us with the might of the buffalo and the courage of the jaguar. We learn because he teaches us and he does not disdain to use the lowly mosquito to impart knowledge to us."

The sight of more than one hundred thousand people praying together brought the descending spirit to those of spirit. "The people" had long realized that they were sharing the stage of life together. They understood that no individual could succeed alone. It was not that individual talents could not shine, but a single individual could not outshine the group. "The people" had come to know long ago that envy could not be the foundation of civilization. They had eliminated envy by giving.

"Never forget that this land is a blessing for all of us. We have traveled the world and bear witness to the end of those who have gone before."

The council fire finished its burn. Tidasi and Tallulah finally had their chance to slip away to be alone. This was the first time that they been alone since Tidasi's return from the sea.

Tidasi looked deeply into the eyes of his wife and said, "The law of love says that I must hold you until we become one. The science of love says that I must arouse and satisfy the thirst created by that love."

"Then hold me and satisfy thirst, my love." Tallulah said in return.

Tidasi sat with Tallulah looking deeply into her deep brown eyes. He touched her soft bronze colored skin. She passed her hand over the locks of his hair. Tidasi wore his hair in the traditional locks that all the descendants of the Olmec wore. It was a tradition among the men to wear seven locks of long hair. His copper colored body complimented that of his wife as he held her gently.

A fire burned inside the sleeping chamber. The thick rugs carpeted the floors and the aura of passion was present as well. Tidasi began to softly massage fragrant oil into the skin of Tallulah. She responded by opening up herself to be receptive to his touches and by kissing him passionately.

The two had no other desire except for one another. During his travels Tidasi had seen many beautiful women, yet this beauty made him long more for Tallulah. She was his other half. She fed him delicacies which he ate from her fingers. Then she pured fragrant oil on his skin and massaged it in sensually. Her aim was only to arouse him to the highest level to which he could be raised. She intended only to bring out the power that was locked deep inside her man.

"I am your love and your lover. I will give to you everything that I have forever," she said to husband.

"And I will give all that I can give, because I am your love and your lover as well. Come close to me and receive the fruit of my passion. Let me give you everything."

There was plenty of oil for both the fire and the love. Tidasi heated the oil to make it warmer. His touch persuaded Tallulah give way, melt, and separate. He made love to his wife and she to her husband.

*****

Nosh, Tidasi, and the rest of the family sat together for breakfast. There was so much food remaining that the feasting could continue for a full week. And some of leftovers would be preserved for later.

The rest of the day would be spent by visiting friends and giving gifts. All the homes were decorated beautifully. The gardens had provided plenty this year. Even the pets were eating well.

Though many foreigners had immigrated to Aztalan "the people" all had taken the same approximate hue. They were of varying shades of olive from light to dark. It was known that the founders of the Anahuac civilization were the Olmec who were brown skinned people.

With this "the people" of Anahuac were not given to color prejudice. They knew that all people were the descendants of the same root and thus all were branches of the same family. Differences were seen as an asset of the human family and anyone who was different was welcomed into the fold.

When the travelers such as the Mauritanians, Iberians, and Asians did arrive seeking trade they were welcomed. Many of them remained and made their homes among "the people". And they in turn became of "the people" as well. Aztalan had been a melting pot many years before.

The land was bountiful and was large enough so allotments could be given to refugees if the need arose. Some allotments of land had been given to settlers in the east who were known as the Mengwe. The Mengwe were considered the brothers to "the people". "The people" was what "the people" of Cahokia and Aztalan called themselves. This was the same name that the Cushites of Africa, including Egypt, referred to themselves. They were all called "the people". Each year a portion of the harvest was set aside to be given to the Mengwe and others. The Mengwe also gave a portion of their harvest to others.

The Mengwe in turn were good neighbors and trading partners with "the people". They provided food from the inland sea of the north. They also provided oil and meat from the harvest of whales from the ocean.

It was the Mengwe who were considered the closes allies and relatives. "The people" of the west were also held in high esteem by "the people". In fact, it was the name "the people" by which all of "the people" of Anahuac went. There was no greater distinction than to be known as the first nation of the Olmec of whom "the people" were descended.

So as long as any immigrants obeyed the law they were welcomed in Aztalan. As long as the law was obeyed there would be was no oppression. The law protected "the people" from themselves.

Chapter 3

*I*t was when the blue-gray wolf and red-brown deer mated that the first Mongol was born. Then out of the cold dark forest of Baikal in Siberia did they come forth. They grew hardy and strong because of the extremes of the environment which they had to endure. The temperatures sometimes plummeted to seventy degrees below zero. They raised themselves up out of a place where the fire of hell was as cold as the freezing burn of ice.

"We will go to the great land called 'Turtle Island' to the east where 'the people' are magicians. It is said that they are able perform miracles. And there is a great river which is feed by other great rivers and the land is rich," said the Great Khan. "We will add their uniqueness to our to our own. We are the most powerful military force that the world has ever seen. We will govern the entire world. We will govern Kemanahuac north and south."

Within Asia there had been a revolution taking place for hundreds of years. Those who had been roped into the darkness of the northern void had broken through. A people developed who were to become the most fantastic military machine ever imagined, the Mongols of Asia. At that time there was no state called Mongolia and the land was inhabited by a people who had somehow began in the Caucasia region north of "The Wall of the Caucasians".

The wall had been built and maintained for eons as a way to keep the barbarians from the north out of civilization. It was through amalgamation that the mankind who were to become Mongols came into being. The Mongols were not of a single specific ethnicity. They were a conglomeration of military and political factions molded under discipline into a complete global empire. The form of government was an absolute monarchy.

The capital of this military might was within the geographic area of what is today called Russia, Mongolia, and parts of China. The leadership of this military might was the paramount ruler, the Great Khan. The apparent reason for the conquest of the world was manifested as tribute to be paid in the form of taxes. The real reason was mankind's subjugation of man. Any nation that did not subjugate itself or tried to withhold tribute was summarily crushed.

It was the Great Mongol Confederation that consisted of what are today called Vikings and Mongols that held dominion. In fact the Vikings and Mongols were the same people. History shows that the Mongols and Vikings occupied the same place at the same time. They were the land and sea versions of the same military machine.

"It is said that 'the people' of 'Turtle Island' are Cushites," spoke the Great Khan. The Great Khan was the absolute ruler of the Mongol vision of the world. The Mongols had only been stopped in Africa by Egypt. Soon they would turn their attention to Anahuac.

At this time "the people" had heard that had Northern Horde that had usurped most of civilization. They also knew that a wall of glacier ice protected them. This was why Anahuac enjoyed relative peace during the early Mongol onslaught. But it was starting to get warm globally and the ice was starting to melt.

"We will give 'the people' of Aztalan the honor of joining our confederation for protection. We will be their closest friends. They can no longer be isolated by ice and seas", the Great Khan continued.

"It is said that 'the people' of Aztalan are possessors of amazing intelligence and technology. They are also known to be very strong," said Batachikan, the closest adviser and prime to the Great Khan.

The Great Khan thought silently to himself, "*What are the estimates?*"

"Turtle Island is very large and there are many people. In addition Anahuac has many allies among the Cushites worldwide. If we make war on them it may come to involve all of the nations of the world," said Batachikan. "We should first offer them the opportunity of joining with us."

"They believe that they are the root of man. They call themselves 'the people' of the first civilization," continued the Great Khan. "How long will it take to subdue Anahuac and the entirety of Kemanahuac?" the Great Khan asked.

"This will take many years. The nations of Anahuac are allied together through bloodlines," Batachikan answered. "However, there is a passage opening in the northwest of Anahuac. There is at present a corridor that will lead us into their midst. We will have to fight 'the people' who defend the coast of the land and the corridor."

"How long will this take?"

"We can push onto the shores and secure a foothold in less than one year. Pushing down the corridor into Anahuac will be more difficult. Unless."

"Unless?" repeated the Great Khan.

"Unless we send the Vikings to assault Anahuac from the opposite flank. This will divert their attention and perhaps give us the time we need to take a foothold on both coasts. The Vikings on the east and the Mongols on the west," said the Batachikan. "We will squeeze them until there is nowhere to go except south."

"This is our plan then," affirmed the Great Khan. "Go to Hiamovi and give him one message. Accepted the patronage of the Great Mongol Confederation or perish."

With these words the course of events that would forever change Anahuac were set in place. The Great Mongol Confederation was not a simple gathering of barbarians who set out to rape, plunder, and eat raw meat. They had perfected the most sophisticated battle tactics that world simply could not resist. They had also perfected bureaucracy. They were very organized.

It was in the technology of warfare that the Northern Horde was in its element. They were superior horsemen, superior archers, and they were the possessors of steel weapons. These were the barbaric descendants of the original Tamahu who had been expelled from civilization so long ago.

Batachikan led his delegation to Aztalan. His expedition would be one of negotiation. He would attempt to contract tribute in the form of trade. All would serve the Mongol Empire. Batachikan knew that a war with Anahuac would be costly on both sides. He also knew that there was the possibility of a world war. "The people" would not stand by and watch the destruction of Aztalan and Cahokia.

"Perhaps it would be more prudent to form an alliance with 'the people' for trade. We will have a better opportunity to gain a foothold in Anahuac. Once we enter as allies we shall never leave," said Batachikan.

"You are right we should attempt to take the Anahuac in intact," said the Great Khan. "All under heaven must submit to the Great Mongol Confederacy".

"It is decided then. Anahuac shall become a part of the Great Mongol Confederacy," agreed Batachikan. "Your word is law, Great Khan."

The Eastern Mongol Army encamped at Lake Baikal awaiting orders to advance across the straight and down through the back door of Anahuac. Five hundred thousand soldiers would be dispatched. Of that number half would be Vikings approaching from the east of Anahuac from Greenland. The Vikings were the Mongol army of the west had subdued Europe with the exception of Iberia. The conquest of Anahuac would be a joint effort of the combined forces of the armies of the east and the west. This would be the greatest military exercise in world history.

Batachikan's and his guard, the warrior brothers Naran and Saran, the Sun and Moon, arrived at the shores of the back door of Anahuac by ship. It was said that the brothers were so fearsome that they alone could stand guard for the Great Khan. They brought with them their supplies for the journey ahead, including well trained horses. Batachikan would be the embodiment of the Great Khan. And his guard pledged filial piety to the Great Khan and to his representative, Batachikan.

It was determined that the staging ground for the assault of the Mongol army would be Vinland, Vancouver Island. The Vikings, the Mongol marines, would provide the logistics for the effort. The Vikings under the leadership of Leif had scouted and mapped the passages from east to west by water. At that time the waters of the north were ice free. Due to their agrarian nature the population of Vinland could be easily subdued without resistance.

The Mongols had been disciplined by the rugged terrain and

harsh climates of their origins. Existence in extremes of temperature sometimes reaching minus seventy degrees or more made the Mongols a strong and hardy people who sympathized little with people who occupied the regions of milder climates of the south. The Mongols were tough. It wasn't the pursuit of comfort that gave rise to the aggressiveness of the Mongols, but it was the pursuit of equanimity.

Batachikan marveled at what he saw. The rivers were darkened by the schools of fish. The herds of animals were boundless. Anahuac was truly the promise land. With each step that the Mongol emissary took he found newness.

"Batachikan," shouted Naran. An unbelievable monster was approaching and bearing down on the emissary.

It was a giant short-faced bear that was truly the king of this domain. It was out searching for its next meal. The giant short-faced bear was the most feared animal in Anahuac. Legends were filled with harrowing stories of the giant short-faced bear feasting on humans. Fortunately its hunting grounds were far to the north.

Naran and Saran went on the offensive against the bear. The bear went on the offensive against them. They employed the same battle tactics that they had used against many adversaries. They used deception and misdirection. Naran charged the animal indirectly by moving in a circular pattern. Saran circled the other flank, and Batachikan stood his ground and moved forward. They had never seen a giant short-faced bear before, and the bear had never encountered Mongols.

Simultaneously, the three fired arrows from their compound bows. The shots ripped through the bear. The warriors shot again and again filling the bear with arrows. He turn to run, but it was in the hot pursuit of the wounded that the Mongols excelled. The bear would not escape this day.

By the end of the encounter the Mongols and their horses were wearing the warm fur of the bear for coats. They wore its claws as ornaments around their necks. And the giant short-faced bear meat would fill their bellies. Batachikan knew that the fiercest beasts in forest of Anahuac would not be the giant short-faced bears but the Great Horde of the Mongols.

"Let this bear be a lesson to all the beasts of Anahuac," shouted Naran to the four winds.

The rich beauty of Anahuac was evident to the expedition as they traveled on horseback. Mongols first met a people called the Makkah, the bearded ones. These people had lived in this area for hundreds of years. They wore the long beards of the Arab seaman who had come long ago trade and settled with them. They practiced the religion of Islam with which the Mongols were familiar. The Makkah maintained a domain of land and sea.

"We come in peace from the Mongol Empire of the Great Khan," Batachikan spoke to the Ku Tu of the Makkah. It was the way of the Mongols to seek acceptance and subjugation of a people first. The Mongols wanted the respect of the civilized.

"Why have you come through the back door?" asked the Makkahan chief.

"The glacier is receding and a passage has opened. This will allow free passage from Asia. We are going to Cahokia."

"The glacier is melting?" the Ku Tu asked in disbelief. There was a great global warming taking place. The worldwide temperatures were rising significantly. This was allowing the migration of people worldwide.

The Makkah knew that this would allow access to Anahuac from the north, the back door. The glaciers had acted as an insulator which protected "the people" from invasion from the north. It was shocking to hear that the natural fortress was now gone and "the people" were vulnerable.

"Cahokia is still a very far journey. We will allow you passage through our lands", said the Ku Tu of the Makkah.

"The Great Khan is offering you the opportunity to join the Great Mongol Confederation. We will bring peace and will be your closest friends," Batachikan spoke for the Great Khan.

"We are of Anahuac. This is as it has always been. We are living in peace."

"We will take your final decision upon our return," Batachikan impressed upon the leader of the Makkah, who only recently return from the council meeting in Cahokia.

Batachikan continued on his journey to Aztalan. With each nation that the emissary of the Great Khan passed he marveled at the grace and efficiency of the society. He saw the infrastructure of the civilization was built around agriculture and industry. He also saw that in the west a series of canals that crisscrossed the landscape.

The emissary of the Great Khan saw that there were large organized farms and agricultural science in place. The Mongols noticed crops that were unknown to them including the potato and the tomato.

He saw that the government of Anahuac did not follow a bureaucratic form of government. Because the laws were few and universal the government could be administered locally. The government as he witness was composed of the common law of the land and individual rights. Batachikan saw the individual peace that each enjoyed.

The Mongols saw that there were horses in Anahuac. The type of horse was similar to that of the Mongols. The indigenous horses were short in height and powerful as were those of the Mongol breed. Batachikan and the warrior brothers could see the utility of the endurance and power of the Anahuac horse. The Mongols instantly deduced that a new breed of powerful military horses could be produced by amalgamating the breeds.

"These horses are more powerful than ours," said Naran.

"I will take one," said Saran as he set out capture a horse.

Naran and Batachikan watched as Saran charged the Anahuac horse. The powerful horse could not be overtaken by the Mongol horse. The horse seemed to be toying with the Mongol. It would let him catch up and then pull away at will. Try as he might Saran could not capture the horse which wanted to remain free.

"The people" of Anahuac sought not to subjugate the animals of the land. There did exist domesticated animals. Animals did, however, enjoy the right of freedom. Each horse was raised from a colt and in essence became a member of "the people". Once the horse was included as a member of society it was under the protection of the law. "The people" did not abuse animals.

By this time the Mongols had reached "the people" of the Missouri. The Missouri were a dark-brown and powerful people. The men were as tall and physically imposing just as their cousins of Cahokia. They were the descendants of the Olmec and Shang amalgamation.

Some men of the Missouri led by "Big Horse" observed the horsemanship of the Mongol. They saw the Saran was an expert rider. However, his horse did not possess the enduring speed of the Anahuac horse. Saran chased in vain. The Mongols maintain a respect for livestock as well, especially the horse. It was the horse that had been the vehicle by which the conquest of Europe and Asia was made.

Batachikan and Naran laughed at the efforts of Saran. Saran then readied an arrow to be fired from his bow. He deftly took aim on the galloping horse. His well trained horse held steady as he took aim.

"Saran," Batachikan called to the warrior. Saran let his arrow go. It was sent flying passed the ear of horse and through the animal's mane. A tuft of hair was cut and lifted into the air as the arrow sailed far ahead. Saran's assault was halted and the horse was allowed to go unharmed.

The men of the Missouri had never before seen the compound bow. This was a completely new and modern technology. They were very impressed with the ability to fire powerful many shots in succession. They were however completely confident in the power and accuracy of the lance and atlatl. Soon word of the visitors and advanced weaponry spread throughout the land.

Batachikan also saw that there was no deceit among "the people". Anahuac was a proper civilization as he had heard. There was a complete infrastructure and government. All of "the people" spoke the same common language, Cushite. They all followed the Law of the One.

The emissary noticed that whenever he saw interaction of "the people" they always dealt honestly with each other. He then learned their weakness. He knew that it would be the honesty of "the people" which would be their end. The Mongols had subjugated and exacted tribute from many honest men. He also knew that all warfare was based on deception. He knew that to be knowledgeable in the ways of the enemy was to gain a step up on that enemy.

As he traveled he told all that he met of the glory of the Mongol

Whispers of a Man 41

Global Empire. He told "the people" of conquest and military might. His guard continued to demonstrate advanced horsemanship and weaponry. They were the most excellent of soldiers. It was in the Mongol army that conscription was for life. It was a blood tax paid for by each family giving one son for the nation. It was this bond of "the people" to the military that gave the nation its might.

Batachikan and his guard were welcomed as guests throughout the land. "The people" now knew of their presence ahead of their arrival. Wherever the Mongols turned they were met with the gentle smiles "the people". The Mongols found themselves in the midst of the sea of "the people". They realized that "the people" were many. They population of Anahuac was well into the tens of millions.

The Mongols saw for themselves the graciousness of "the people". They saw that "the people" practiced spirit as the guiding principle in their lives. The Mongols had come to realize that "the people" had perfected a harmonious relationship with their environment. They were so unlike the barbarians from the north who sought conquest and the subduing of the resources of the Earth as virtue.

The Mongols came to be known by their horses. As they moved they often startled "the people". Batachikan restrained the aggressive tendencies of his Naran and Saran. They would commit no offense against the law of the land or "the people". However, the Mongols saw "the people" as weak due to their unaggressive nature.

"These are weak men. They are not fit to occupy this great land," said Naran.

"It is true they are weak. They have not made a challenge to strangers who travel unrestricted through their lands," said Saran.

"They maybe unaggressive, but this is not to be mistaken for weakness. They appear to be a people who are just. We must not make the mistake of not knowing them," Batachikan countered. "I do not sense weakness within them.

"We can never treat them as equals with Mongol soldiers," Naran said.

"We have not seen their warriors yet," said Batachikan.

"I think that they do not have warriors," said Saran.

"It is a wise people who do not display their weapons of war," said Batachikan.

"They are large and meek," said Saran.

"They are gentle people, but extremely powerful," Batachikan added.

Still Batachikan could see what his men could not see. He did not see "the people" as weak. He saw them as content. He knew that as his party made its way deeper into Anahuac the more that his presence would be known. Soon the Mongols came to a great river, the Mississippi. Across the river they could see a Great Pyramid glistening in the distance.

Batachikan, Naran, and Saran stood in awe of what they saw. Cahokia was the most magical and beautiful city that they could have ever imagined. They saw boats and barges moving on the Mississippi. They could not have imagined the picture of a civilized nation so far away.

Now the first representatives of the Great Mongol Confederacy were witness to the marvel of the Cushite nation in Anahuac. What they witnessed from the opposite shore of the river astounded them. To witness this marvel in the forest and grass made them believe in magic. They began to think that perhaps the stories of magicians were true.

Then as if out of nowhere there stood before them men of the color of fired bronze and of giant proportion. Hundreds of men of "the people" of Aztalan and Cahokia had come out to meet the visitors. "The people" were fully aware of the presence and journey of the Mongols. It was as Batachikan had sensed "the people" were fully aware of that he was coming to Cahokia.

Chapter 4

The Mongol delegation entered Cahokia as honored guest. Batachikan was welcomed as a visiting ambassador of the Mongol Confederation. He and his guard were taken to a place of rest and given food and drink. They were welcomed in the way that all the dignitaries who visited Aztalan were welcomed.

Hiamovi assigned escorts to act as guides and provide for the needs of the guests. He allowed them to rest from their long journey from the other side of the world before greeting them. Nosh would represent him at the first meeting.

"I am the representative of the Great Khan whom all under heaven submit," Batachikan stated as his opening.

"Welcome to Cahokia. We welcome you as delegates and guest from the Mongol Confederation," responded Nosh. Tidasi, Heluska, Enapay, Cheveyo, and Kitchi accompanied Nosh in his welcoming party.

"We have come to share the glory of the Great Mongol with your people. We have come to ask that you embrace friendship. We are extending to you our hand and an invitation to become a part of the Great Mongol," said Batachikan.

"We accept your friendship as we extend our own and welcome you our home," said Nosh. "If you have any needs you have only to ask."

"We wish to speak to Ku Tu Hiamovi," said Batachikan.

"Hiamovi welcomes you to Cahokia, and he will personally welcome you after you have rested."

Naran and Saran sat silently observing Tidasi, Heluska, and the others and were observed by them. Tidasi and Heluska had long ago had heard and seen firsthand how perceived Mongol friendship could change into malevolence. Tidasi and Heluska towered over Naran and Saran. The Mongol soldiers held the representatives of Cahokia in disdain. Enapay, Cheveyo, and Kitchi smiled as they always did.

The Mongols entered into the heart of Cahokia. "The people" looked on in wonder at the strangely dressed Asians. The style of the Mongols was disheveled and vulgar. They did not observe the formalities of manners and courtesy. "The people" continued in the gentle way as an example to the guests. Batachikan continued to observe the mannerism and polite way of "the people".

"We have come to you to extend the hand and embrace of friendship," Batachikan said to Hiamovi.

"We welcoming you to our country. And we return the embrace of friendship of the Great Khan," said Ku Tu Hiamovi.

"What do you seek in addition to friendship?" Nosh spoke sensing that there was something more to the visit than was apparent.

"The Great Khan extends an invitation to join the Great Mongol," answered Batachikan.

"Join the Great Mongol?" repeated Hiamovi.

"It is an honor," assured Batachikan.

"And we are honored at the invitation," replied Nosh.

"Then you accept," assumed Batachikan.

"'The people' of Aztalan submit only to the One. And our law forbids submitting to any other. We maintain the adherence to the law as set forth by Tehuti and maintained by the Olmec. To follow any other than this is unacceptable. You may stay among 'the people' as long as you wish. You should observe and follow the law while you are in our midst," stated Hiamovi.

"We will obey your law," agreed Batachikan.

"The people" remained very curious about the new visitors who were now known throughout the land. The discipline of the Mongols was very apparent. Naran and Saran observed the martial practices of "the people". They could see that the stature and continence of "the people" was a magnitude larger than the average Mongol. However, the Vikings stood equal in stature to the men of Cahokia.

"The people" had not yet met the red bearded Vikings.

Naran and Saran practice daily their marital skills under the watchful eye of Tidasi and Heluska. Though vulgar the Mongols were without fear and conducted themselves with graceful fluidity. Their excellence with the compound bow and sword were unequaled by anyone in Aztalan. They also practiced a form of grappling.

"Would you like to join us in training," Enapay invited Naran and Saran to grapple.

Naran stepped into the circle where matches were to take place. Enapay stood before Naran smiling. The two prepared to grapple.

Naran smiled his sinister smile at Enapay and said, "Sure."

Saran laughed aloud as well. How could this boy defeat a solider of Naran status. Naran made an attempt to move first, but Enapay move before he tried to move. Naran's attack met nothing but air as he went flying through air and crashing into the ground. Enapay circled smiling. Enapay's senses were heightened as were all the grapplers of Aztalan. It was said they could feel the air moving with the intentions of their opponents to move.

Naran became hot in his excitement as he became hostile in preparation for his assault. Enapay calmed his demeanor more. Naran's tactic was simply hot pursuit. He would overwhelm Enapay with power, speed, and strength. Enapay could not be caught in the grasp of Naran. Naran appeared to be trying to catch a slippery snake. Enapay appeared and disappeared suddenly in places where Naran was not expecting him to be.

Tidasi, Heluska, Cheveyo, and Kitchi stood silently observing the Mongol technique which was considerably more violent than their own. Enapay easily countered the attacks of Naran. Naran began to augment his attack with kicks and punches. His assault was still to no avail. At this point the grappling technique of Cahokia was superior to the Mongol.

However, Naran's assault was relentless. He continued to attack with impunity. At one point in his attempt at assault Enapay captured his neck in a choke. Naran would not relent until Enapay had put him completely asleep.

"Naran, Naran," Saran said while shaking his brother awake.

"What happened," Naran sat up embarrassed. He looked at his

brother in humiliation. "I am going to killed that snake."

Now the Mongol soldiers were beginning to see that the grappling technique of "the people" was superior to their own. They also found themselves appreciating the skill and technique of the grapplers of Cahokia. The Mongols became a daily fixture at the training sessions of the grapplers.

They soon came to realize that it was movement in the vein of tranquility that flowed effortlessly as the great river in which power was gathered, store, and released. The Mongols soon came to see strength and weakness with a different perspective. They came to see the nonaggressive nature of "the people" was far different than a lack of strength. They simply could not overpower or intimidate the grapplers of the Cahokia. The bravery of "the people" matched the tenacity and relentlessness of the Mongols. The grapplers of Cahokia were unafraid of loss or injury.

Mongol soldiers then begin to demonstrate their forte which was horsemanship and weaponry. Their compound bow was a weapon that had not been developed in Aztalan. Its power and reach gave the them an advantage in long distance, accuracy, and timing. The rapid fire advantage of the compound bow was due to the thumb draw technique which they employed.

They also utilized the curved sword, mace, and ax. It was in advance weaponry combined with extraordinary horsemanship that the Mongol superiority to "the people" stood obvious. These tools combine with a fierce and aggressive demeanor made the Mongol a fearsome fighting machine.

This disadvantage was apparent to both "the people" and the Mongols. There was no intention to copy the compound bow. There had been no war in Aztalan since the time of the Maya, and to use the weapon for the hunt would give an unfair advantage and detracted from the spirit of the hunt. Therefore, "the people" ignored the compound bow technology.

"Their weapons are superior to our own," Tidasi said to Heluska.

"We are the physically superior to them," added Heluska.

"Physical superiority is not necessarily an advantage," countered Tidasi.

"They are very tenacious," said Enapay.

"They appear to be very dangerous," Heluska sensed.

"I feel the same. I don't feel friendship from them," said Cheveyo.

"What do they want?" asked Kitchi.

"We will see," said Tidasi.

The Mongol delegates observed all manners of other advances in use among "the people". They observed the advance agriculture and animal husbandry. They saw that "the people" did not conquer the land in the same sense that the Mongols conquered lands. "The people" saw that the enslavement and subjugation of the lands did not empower them with more control. They perceived that it was the Great Spirit that provided everything and they saw that there could not be subjugation without the consequence of retribution.

"Their weapons are poor," said Saran to Batachikan.

"We are far more superior as soldiers," added Naran.

"This is not a warlike people. They are pacifists and disdain war. Which is a good thing because it is better to take a nation intact, and it is better to take a city without destroying it," said Batachikan. "Be aware that because they do not make weapons of destruction does not mean that they are inferior men. They are without fear. This makes them accepting of death."

"It makes them weak," Saran said disgustingly.

"There is much knowledge here. They are physically imposing and very fit. They are as large as Vikings," Batachikan stated.

"Ask Naran about this," laughed Saran remembering the grappling match with Enapay.

"They do have some skills," agreed Naran

Retribution was indistinguishable from the law and nature of the Great Spirit. "The people" enjoyed the solace of balance that the adherence to the law of the One afforded. The Mongols began to see the correlation and relationship of the law, land, and the One with which "the people" blended. "The people" were a part of the land and the law was the maintenance of the interval that connected each to the land. Balance was an equation that precluded a disharmonious relation with the environment.

The thing the Mongols noticed most about "the people" was the way that they employed purposefulness in everything that they did. Batachikan, Naran, and Saran saw "the people" were not spiritual, but they were spirit. They saw the sincerity and unpretentiousness of each action. They also saw the way that each of "the people" went about their tasks sincerely.

"I do not see houses of worship in Cahokia," Batachikan said to Hiamovi.

"We do not build houses of worship as others do because we do not wish to learn to quarrel with God," said Hiamovi.

"Do you tax your people?" asked Batachikan.

"We have no need to take from "the people". All of us give whatever we do not need. And we give assistance and kindness wherever it is needed. "

"Is there ownership of the land?"

"We chose to remain close to the Great Spirit and treat the Earth and all that dwell thereon with respect. So in the sense that you are speaking there is no ownership of land, or you may say that we all own it."

"How is it that your government is rich?"

"It is the Great Spirit who is rich. We benefit from this wealth which is provided for all of us."

"Do you work?" asked Batachikan.

"We all work," answered Hiamovi.

"The Great Khan would not sully his hands with work."

"Let him who would move the world first move himself."

The Mongols studied "the people" in all their manners. It began to become clear that "the people" were natural people. The circle of life began and ended in the same place.

"There is no death only the change of worlds," Hiamovi said to Batachikan.

Batachikan saw the strength in the way of life of "the people". He saw that basis of living according to the law was the strength of "the people". He could sense that this harmonious relationship could not be improved upon. He began to see that they never took too much or gave too little.

Naran and Saran also studied the way of "the people". They saw the methods of hunting as inefficient. They saw the lance and atlatl as primitive weaponry.

"Why do you use these inefficient weapons?" asked Naran.

"We take only enough," answered Tidasi.

"We can take many buffalo," said Saran.

"We do not need more," said Heluska.

"We can kill from a distance," said Naran.

"It is easy to be brave from a distance," said Tidasi.

Each citizen of Cahokia went about their daily business without need for external motivation. There were no overseers employed on any projects. There were no commands being barked. The motivation to succeed was inspired by the sense of community. When the time for harvest came Hiamovi and Nosh also took to the fields.

Hiamovi, Nosh and Batachikan walked far into land. Naran, Saran, Heluska, Tidasi, and his brothers accompanied them. Batachikan saw the advance technology that was employed in the field of horticulture. "The people" of Kemanahuac and particularly Aztalan had developed and produced many varieties of crops which they were exporting to the world.

"The people" appeared exceptionally healthy. Batachikan saw that this was due to the hygienic practices that were in place. Waste was recycled and excrement was kept out of the ecosystem. "The people" bathed regularly and oral hygiene was practiced. Natural healing and herbal medicine was practiced as a profession.

"Do you maintain a standing army?" asked Batachikan.

"No, we do not maintain an army in the way that you do," Hiamovi answered.

"How will you protect yourselves from assault from the outside?"

"Why do we have need for protection?" asked Nosh.

"A nation which does not prepare its defenses will fall sooner or later."

"We do not have a standing army. However, each of us is taught to defend this land," said Hiamovi.

"How can you prevent invasion if you don't have a friend like the Great Mongol Confederacy," said Batachikan.

"If we are invaded by an outside force then the Earth itself will swallow our enemies. To conceive to invade is simple but to withdraw will not be. There can be no victory over a fearless people. Only endless war," said Hiamovi.

Batachikan began to realize the nature of bravery. He was beginning to understand the dilemma that the nature of the bravery of "the people" would present to the Mongols. Engagement and invasion could result in an endless war. The thought of war without end was not even for the Mongols something that was desirable. It was an impossible dream that could turn into a Thanatos nightmare.

Hiamovi could see that the idea of a war without end was sending trepidations through Batachikan. And Batachikan knew that Hiamovi knew this. It was aggression that drove the Great Horde onward. It was their aggressive tenaciousness which gave them glory. Now it was their life's blood that Hiamovi was recognizing as an Achilles heel. As war was their heaven it might also become their hell.

The Mongol Confederation was not something new. It was the continuation of a line descending from Caucasius and the Tamahu. The Northern Hordes had grown up through the Hittites, Scythians, Avars, Turkic, and finally, the Mongols. All these nations were the amalgamation of the barbaric Hordes of Caucasia and ethnically mixed. These seemingly diverse nations had originated in the dawn of their beginnings in the Anatolia region north of the Caucasius Wall.

"Although your confederation is vast our country is also vast. An invasion would be unwise," said Hiamovi.

He was telling Batachikan that to invade Anahuac would be to be swallowed up and self-immolation. The country was simply too large to invade and conquer from the other side of the world.

Hiamovi and Nosh understood that Aztalan could not be conquered only destroyed. Batachikan knew that to destroy a nation was inferior to taking it intact.

"By uniting with the Great Mongol all "the people" of the world can benefit," said Batachikan.

"We have not asked to be united with the Great Mongol. You serve your Great Khan while we serve the Great Spirit," said Nosh. "This is the fundamental difference between us."

"This is why we cannot become a part of the Mongol Confederacy," said Hiamovi.

"We do not wish to invade your nation. We wish you to join with us as friends. Please consider this. We want only trade with you," Batachikan said.

"Trading with us does not require a threat," said Nosh.

"We do not threaten. We are asking you to embrace us as we embrace you."

"We are your friends, but we are also a sovereign nation," said Hiamovi.

"The Great Mongol only seeks to bring order to the world. We are offering a better way for mankind. A new world order."

"We are the descendants of the original man," said Nosh.

"The old ways must change. This old religion that you practice is now the religion of magicians. These old ways are falling all over the world. You are the last of the first civilization people."

"Is this not enough reason to preserve the last of a kind?" asked Hiamovi.

"Everything changes," replied Batachikan.

"As much as things change the more that they remain the same," continued Hiamovi. "It is the natural way for correction to happen. Mankind will find that the way of conquest cannot endure. And empires rise and fall. Our ancestors saw the rise of mankind since its foundation. We are all descendants of the same ancestors. We already live in you and you in us. We are already one people. This is why we embrace you. You are our cousins."

"Then it is more proper for you to join with your family, and to avoid a family quarrel," said Batachikan.

Batachikan could hear a sound being carried by the wind. The melody of the sound penetrated to into the center of his being.

"What is that sound?" asked Batachikan.

"That is Hiawatha," answered Nosh.

"That sound is the most beautiful sound that I have ever heard. What is it?'

"It is his playing of the flute," said Hiamovi.

"Who is Hiawatha?" asked Batachikan.

"He is a teacher," said Hiamovi.

"He gives guidance. His song is carried by the winds to all lands," added Nosh.

"It is the silent sound that is heard by all. You hear it whether you know it or not," said Hiamovi.

"I would like to meet the source of this beautiful sound," said Batachikan.

"Let us follow the wind," said Hiamovi.

They followed the sound that left its trail on the wind. The closer to the source of the sound they moved the more peace moved toward them. Batachikan had never known tranquility and peace that he sensed before. He had learned to discipline his mind. He had heard peace mentioned as it related to the absence of war. He had never realized peace as solitude that was found within and in harmony with others. Where he had come from everything was so noisy. There was no peace.

Hiawatha sat producing the sounds that they heard. He played the interchange of the internal breaths flowing into the outgoing breaths. The deer, buffalo, and birds were enchanted by his melody. They stood close by. The incense of fruits and flowers perfumed the air. Hiawatha continued to play.

"Hiamovi, Nosh" Hiawatha greeted with a smile. "Welcome."

"It has been too long since we have visited you," said Hiamovi.

"Your song has drawn us to you again," added Nosh.

"I am happy that you can still hear it," said Hiawatha.

"It is wonderful," said Batachikan.

"Let us smoke," Hiawatha offered his pipe.

They group sat in a circle together. Each of them could see into the eyes of the other. They sat to listen and to smoke. Batachikan listened to the freedom song that was played. Hiamovi passed the pipe to Batachikan while Hiawatha played.

"What is it that we smoke?" asked Batachikan.

"It is hemp."

"Hemp," repeated Batachikan.

"We use it for many things. Our clothing is made from hemp. We make medicines and fuel. And we eat and smoke the leaves and flowers. There are more than one hundred uses of hemp for the benefit of everyone."

"Yes it is very beautiful. I am calm," Batachikan was starting to let go.

Whispers of a Man

Naran and Saran also took their turns smoking the pipe. They began to relax as well. Soon they started to laugh. They began to laugh uncontrollably. Tidasi and the others started laughing too.

"I feel peaceful," said Naran.

"Yes, me too," agreed Saran. "We are smoking the peace pipe." Everyone started laughing again at Saran's comment.

"I think that I am going jump in the pond," said Naran. Then he got up, went over, and jumped into the pond. He was shortly followed by Saran. The two had never felt so much at ease. Then Kitchi and Cheveyo joined them. The four performed their best antics.

"How do you produce these primitive sounds?" Batachikan asked.

"Primitive? You hear or see something for the first time and regard it as primitive," answered Hiawatha. "The sun renews itself daily and fades away each night. Do you see it as primitive? Because is derived from the base does not mean that it is primitive. The sound that you hear is primal not primitive.

"Primal? What is that?"

"When I play this flute it produces the sweetness that is heard on the wind. The wind is carried to the ends of the Earth to calm the primitive. And when you hear it peace envelopes you," said Hiawatha.

"I am calmed by this sound," said Batachikan.

"When you return to your home listen to the whisper of the flute for it will follow you always in your travels. It will be a reminder of the ripple in the lake of tranquility that is you. Try to still the ripple."

"Tell me about your religion," asked Batachikan.

"Our religion consists of a humble admiration of the illimitable Great Spirit who reveals himself in the slight details which we are able to perceive with our frail and feeble minds," said Hiawatha.

Batachikan smoked with Hiamovi, Nosh, Tidasi, Heluska, Enapay, and Hiawatha. They smoked before the fired that burned and Hiawatha told the story of the flute and what its sound meant.

"It is not the sound of the flute which is carried on the wind, but the wind which is motivated by the sound of the flute," said Hiawatha.

"How is this?" asked Batachikan.

"You notice the sound but feel the breeze. The flute is the motivation of the wind to carry this song. This is why on a night far away if you listen quietly you will hear my song. We are reaching out to you so that you may know of us. We are talking to you in your dreams while you sleep. This is so that when you awaken you will find solace. When you awakened on this day did you awake to bliss?"

"My sleep was restful," said Batachikan. "My nights here have been most restful."

"And your dreams?"

"I did dream of different things. I found myself walking in a field that was unencumbered by chaos. And free from strife."

"Freedom from internal strife and inner conflict," said Hiawatha.

"What inner conflict?" asked Batachikan.

"Aggression."

"Warfare is of vital importance to the state," said Batachikan.

"Peace is of vital importance to 'the people'."

"If we did not expand we would stagnate. And another would replace us," said Batachikan.

"Do you fear replacement?"

"We must maintain the Great Mongol."

"You fear loss of something that is uncertain. You fear replacement and that is why move on your neighbors."

The others continued to sit smoke and listen to Hiawatha and Batachikan exchange. Batachikan was very much taken with Hiawatha. Hiawatha continued to play his flute.

"He is the son of the son. He is of the many sons that have come to us," said Hiamovi

"Son of sons?" asked Batachikan.

"These are those who come periodically to us give guidance and correction from the deviation from the path."

"A prophet?" asked Batachikan.

"A teacher," answered Nosh.

"Is this his work?"

"He is Hiawatha," replied Hiamovi.

"When you work you are a flute through whose heart the whispering of the hours turns into music," said Hiawatha.

"Should we all work or should the elite rule without labor," asked Batachikan.

Hiawatha looked up from his playing and into the eyes of Batachikan and answered, "To love life through labor is to be intimate with life's inmost secret. And the elite must show the love of work. They are the ones who put more love into their labors. Work is love made visible."

A small deer approached unafraid and stood next to Batachikan. The Mongol sat silently as the deer nozzle next to him. The deer was unafraid.

"How is it that this animal approaches men?" asked a squeamish Batachikan. He was a man who was used to being feared. Now a deer was unafraid of him.

"He knows from the sound that peace is here and he will come to no harm," said Hiawatha.

"We do not kill for sport," added Nosh.

"What about for meat?"

"If our intention was to take his life he would not have approached us. He knows that in this place there is peace to all, especially for him. We cannot expect him to live in fear for his entire life. This small deer must have someplace where he can walk among man and not fear. So he comes among friends."

"You are friends with a deer?"

"We live in harmony with all creatures," said Hiawatha.

Batachikan had never known men who behaved in this strange way before. Was it proper for men to treat all things as one and to disdain from harming all life? How could man raise above the animals if he took them as equal with himself. Could man move and not step on the ant?

Batachikan could see that there was harmony and peace in this place. What about outside of this place? The Great Mongol was far removed from this. Deer did not approach, nor did any other animals. Man did not approach. Order was maintained through discipline. And that which was undisciplined was cut off and cast aside. In the inner reality of a fantasy the truth could be anything that you wanted it to be. In the world of the Great Mongol this mind was trampled under the foot of the Mongol Horde.

"I am hungry," said Naran.
"Me too," said Saran.
And Hiawatha continued to play his song on the winds.

Chapter 5

*O*ut of the cold dark abyss of the northern void they stood chiseled out of the ice. From the frozen wasteland they had gathered. Neither frost nor wind could cause them to shiver, and from the exposure to the subzero temperatures they did not wince. They were the original abominable snowmen.

They lay encamped at Greenland. Thousands of them gathered at two points, one in the east and the other in the west. They would lead the incursion into east Anahuac. A front would be established in the sparsely populated eastern wilderness. Their other role would be as logistics support for the offensive operations in the west.

These were the Vikings, the marines of the Mongol Horde. These were the descendants of those from the region that lay between the Black and Caspian seas north of the Caucasius Wall. They were from the line of the original wielders of the iron battle-axes.

"Another battle, and this time we will take the heads of some dark skinned savages from Anahuac," yelled Leif who was in command of the Viking regiment.

"Sharpen your blades and make ready," roared Iggle.

They had done reconnaissance throughout the northern territories of Anahuac. They had charted all the rivers and waterways that existed. The long shallow bottom boats that they used were perfect for maneuvering through the Mississippi Waterway System.

They had been ordered to stage under to their leader the red bearded Leif. The Vikings had come to be distinguished and known by their red beards. These were among the largest of mankind. The mere mention of them was the caused of fear for those who inhabited the Northern Hemisphere. They were even known to have made excursions into South Kemanahuac. They were among the best seaman in the world. Their skill as seaman rivaled those of Aztalan.

From time to time they assume the role of merchant marines for the Great Mongol. However, their primary mission was as marines, a land and sea force that was more than formidable.

The Vikings had been dispatched by the Great Khan shortly after he had sent his emissary Batachikan to Cahokia. The Great Khan was not under the assumption that "the people" would voluntarily accept the subjugation to the Great Mongol. It was the way of the Mongols to prepare for all contingencies and to occupy a land either through acquiescence or invasion. Either way Aztalan was to become a part of the Great Mongol Confederacy. Occupation of Greenland as an operation was begun early because the global warming that was taking place made the island subcontinent hospitable. It had become an unseasonably subtropical and had become over grown with vegetation and trees.

The Viking setup encampments and summarily began strip mining operations. Within months of their arrival most of the trees had been cut down. And all the animals had been slaughtered. All the resources of the land now belonged to the Great Khan. The Vikings were as feared by those who inhabited coast as much as those of the steeps feared the Mongol army of the land.

While the delegation from the Great Mongol spoke of peace with Anahuac the Northern Horde prepared for assault and war. The soldiers drilled daily practicing the landing tactics which made for the sudden appearances for which the Vikings were famous. Again and again the soldiers trained in inhuman conditions. The Vikings were the most battle tested and hardened marine forces in the world.

Unknown to "the people" of Anahuac they had come into full occupation of the Northern Void long ago. It was the Vikings you were the first to find a way through the northern passage that now existed due to the receding glaciers. From the perspective of the Great Mongol the world was not divided into east and west, but was subdivided according to north and south. And the Great Mongol sat on top of the world.

Whispers of a Man

Back and forth did the Vikings transverse the Northern Void into Aztalan and through to Vinland. At Vinland they had lay claim and held a foothold in Anahuac as they did in Greenland. They now sat at the entrances to three doors; north, east, and west. The Great Mongol had conceived to let "the people" escape to the south in abandonment of their homes and lands.

Another important reason for the avoidance of the south was that "the people" would become fully aware of the plan for invasion and would immediately act to repel the incursion. The Great Mongol did not ascent to world domination by employing haphazard tactical strategies. The chain of command and bureaucracy was impeccable. The strategic apparatus of the Mongol Hoard was so opaque as to be considered mysterious. It was never a practice of the Mongols to ever allow an enemy to prepare in any way for an attack. Therefore, an enemy would have to prepare in all places at once. Once the Mongols had employed this tactic then an enemy had lost before a battle had taken place.

The Great Horde would simply appeared and disappeared without a trace. This was the reason for the mystery surrounding the origins and organization of the Mongol Confederation. All warfare is based on deception. It was the strategy of the Mongol Hoard to put themselves beyond defeat. Now they waited for the opportunity to defeat the enemy.

"To secure ourselves against defeat is in our own hands, but the opportunity to defeat the enemy is provided by them," said Leif.

"We will crush our enemies because we are superior in every way. And to a man we are the most fearsome fighting force in the world," Iggle gloated. "Those Cushies are going to feel the cut of our axes."

Leif continued to drive his men on, "Train harder you pathetic dogs." Each word was barked, growled, and snarled. Speaking in an intelligible way not a Viking strong suit, they understood barking better.

There would be no emissaries coming from the Vikings. The Vikings were not diplomats. They existed at the discretion of the Great Khan. Victory was assured them in life and death. Victory meant glory to the Mongol Confederation and death meant Valhalla.

In Valhalla they would be with Odin. Odin was none other than the world-famous Djehuti, Thoth, and Tehuti the Ethiopian sage of old. The Vikings mythology was based on, steeped in, and in fact was the worship of the ancient Ethiopians as gods. It was the drive to strive to the level of the mastery of the builders of civilization that drove them on with impunity. They were the direct descendants of exiled ones from Africa that had been roped into Europe.

The ancient Ethiopians were of such importance in the development of the Caucasius religious systems that an entire pantheon of gods was created. Over time these gods acquired the physical characteristics of those of the Northern Void.

"By Odin, the ability to defeat the enemy means taking the offensive," Leif spoke of the glory of battle. "Defense shows the lack of strength while attacking shows a superabundance of strength."

Leif was the most fitting of soldiers. He understood that on defense it would seemed that his marines were hiding in the most secret of the recess of the Earth. Yet in attack his marines would appear as a flash from the heavens. His army maintained the ability to protect itself and on the other hand could take complete victory.

Knowing the things that everyone could discern was not a special gift. From a distance the strategy blended opaque and no outsider could fathom the tactics. It was the clever fighter who not only won the war but did it with ease. Therefore the Vikings would seek no reputation for wisdom or credit for courage.

"We make no mistakes in battle. We will put ourselves in the position where defeat is impossible," Leif told his men. "This means that we conquer an enemy that is already defeated."

It was victorious battle that the Vikings lived for. They would seek battle only after victory had been won. This disposition separated the Mongol Horde from those destined for defeat. Those destined for defeat fought first and afterward sought victory. Leif commanded his men with strict discipline. Therefore he maintained in his grasp and the power to control success. Far from barbarous in logistics the Northern Horde understood and adhered to method and discipline. In this way was the Great Mongol able to control success.

"Where do we stand logistically?" Leif questioned his second-in-command, Iggle.

"We have taken the measurements," Iggle answered. "We have reckoned the terrain that we will face as we move forward."

"And of the calculations?" Leif asked.

"We have calculated the numbers of provisions that will be necessary. It is a balance that must be of essence in this campaign."

"Speak of calculation relating to victory," ordered Leif.

"We can conclude that ours will be a victorious army. It will be as a mountain compared to a pebble," Iggle responded.

It was the way of the Vikings of the Northern Horde to plan well and not give the enemy the slightest hope of resistance or victory. The calculations seemed to insure that the Great Mongol was assured of annexing Anahuac.

"Victory can be obtained in one fell swoop," mused Leif.

The soldiers continued to train for the planned invasion. Over and over the Vikings gamed to eliminate all doubt and to mitigate all risks. They reconciled the existing contingencies. And like all warriors of the Great Horde they trained under inhuman conditions. They would conduct war games and maneuvers in the extremes of winter. Leif wanted the weak and weary to fall by the wayside before the battle for Anahuac.

Only the strongest would get the honor of going on this excursion. The most harden would be given the honor of killing or dying for the Great Mongol. The weak would not gain Valhalla. The Vikings lived by this code. Each of them sharpened his tools and weapons of war. The soldiers all knew and love the life that they lived. To live and die as a Viking was the great ambition that each of them sought to fulfill.

On the cold night the men would drink Mead, a honey alcohol drink. They would eat a diet which was composed of almost one-hundred percent meat. They would drink the wine which was brought back from Vinland.

It was battle for which they lived. If an argument turned violent then it would be settled by individual combat. To the victor belonged the life of the loser. The warriors serving under Leif had all reached legendary status in name. There was Olaf the Stout, Ivar the Bones, Erik the Blood Ax, Forten the Skull Splitter, and the most notorious of these soldiers was Iggle the Scowler. It was these men and especially Iggle that help to give reputation to the Vikings.

Life of a Viking warrior was fraught with strife from the beginning. As infants they had to measure up. If an infant was deformed or deemed weak then it was thrown into the sea. The life lived by the Vikings appeared in every aspect hard and brutal in opposition to that of Anahuac.

The Vikings sat drinking and singing. Their singing could be compared to the howling of wolves. The sounds that they emitted chased away all beast from their midst. Only their wolfhounds could bear to hear their terrorizing warbling.

"You two are behaving like old women," said Leif to Magnus and Heming. "You are making me ashamed to be a Viking." The two drunkened Vikings glared angrily at each other.

"Stop bickering like two old women. Put it to the ax and the sword," Iggle said, wanting to see some blood spilled as the evening's entertainment.

"The ax and the sword," the other soldiers began to chant drunkenly.

"By Odin, today you shall enter Valhalla," howled Magnus the Skull Crusher to Heming the Fire Ax. The two enormous Vikings stood before each other with shields, sword, and ax at the ready. The pair of red bearded Vikings circled each other, and breathing out the fire of intensity and intention. Heming swung his iron ax at his adversary with intention of destruction. Their eyes burned through the eye-holes in their helmets like red hot charcoal embers. They were killing machines poised to kill.

The others watched the battle in anticipation and excitement. Magnus took his turn with his mighty sword. The two had fought side by side in many battles and each had saved the life of the other more than once. Today the Mead and bloody meat was speaking through them. The sounds of their blows against each other echoed in the wind and resounded with the soldiers. To stand in this place as brave before one's peers was second only to standing side by side with them in battle.

"Embarrass me will you. We will see about that," an angry Magnus barked.

"Me embarrass you? You embarrass me. I going to have your

Whispers of a Man

head," Heming rebutted.

Magnus and Heming gave no quarter as they attempted to dispatch the other. They maintained no quality of mercy. Each blow was struck with the intention to kill. Magnus swung his mighty sword intending to split the body of Heming into halves. The sounds of heavy metal on metal strike resounded in the night. Heming's shield was split down the center by the force of the blow.

Again Magnus came toward Heming. Heming moved with great agility for a man of his size. Magnus attacked his shieldless advisory. Heming ducked low moving into a roll while swinging his own battle-ax as he rolled. Magnus could hardly feel the blow that took his leg off from the knee down. Heming completed his rolled and followed up by bring his ax down and through the top of the head of Magnus. Magnus lay in a bloody pool of snow with his head split asunder. The Vikings cheered their comrades. They cheered Heming for the superb way in which he fought. They also cheered Magnus who had found his way into Valhalla. This was the way of the Vikings, fearless in life and in death.

"He was my best friend," sulked Heming much later after the drunkenness had worn off. "I will never drink again."

"It wasn't the Mead, boy," said Iggle. "It was those damn Cushies."

"Huh."

"Yes, they are the reason why you are here in the first place. So don't blame yourself. Put the blame where it rightfully belongs."

"Yes, I see now. They killed Magnus not me."

"There you go, boy. Now have another drink," Iggle reassured Heming and passed him the Mead.

Magnus was given the highest honor that a Viking could receive. He was given a cremation burial in a flaming Viking boat. His body was laid on a platform on the deck of the boat. Surrounding his body were his possessions and gifts that would accompany him on his journey to the great meat hall in Valhalla. His favorite dog was sacrificed so it would also accompany Magnus.

Heming led the funeral procession. He cried at the loss of his closest friend. He realized that it was the will of the gods that had determined whose death was next. Even if that determination was alcohol induced. Heming placed his ax next to Magnus and took up

Magnus' sword in its place. He was determined to carry it in battle in Anahuac. He vowed that many would fall by the sword of Magnus as expiation for causing the two friends to be in this place in the first place.

All the Vikings were more motivated by the loss of Magnus. They sat drinking Mead and singing praises to his name. They would sit and sing throughout the nights and train throughout the days until the order to march was given. After some time all the blame for the death of Magnus lay with Anahuac. If it had not been for the impending war then the Vikings would not have been there for Magnus to be killed.

"It is the fault of the savages from Anahuac," said a grieving and crying Heming. "They have caused me to kill my best friend. I will make ornaments from their bones. Their skulls shall hang in the meat hall as trophies."

The soldiers continued to eat, drink, sing with tears flowing. They were indeed the rhythmless nation. They sharpened their blades on grinding wheels. Then the silhouettes of ships approached the shores. Like a long serpent and a raven of the wind was the sudden appearance of the crafts. Those aboard the longboats wore the coats of bear or wolf skins. These who were aboard the vessels were the most feared of all Vikings, the Berserkers. They had been dispatched to be under the command of Leif.

The Berserkers were known to overrun all that stood before them and they were the dread to those who dare to try to stand. The other Vikings welcomed them with more singing and more Mead. Animals were killed and their carcasses hung in the open air. It was a horrid site to all but the Vikings to see the mutilated bodies of dead animals everywhere.

When a Viking wanted meat he would simply hack off apiece and eat it raw, or he throw it in the fire if he wanted it a little charred. Most preferred the taste of blood. Meat was served in the windowless meat hall. The air inside was filled with smoke and the walls were black with soot. To the Vikings there was no greater joy than to eat and drink in the great meat hall with his comrades.

The Berserkers told stories of conquests of nations and of men. They told stories of heroes and champions. They told not only of battles with men but they told of battles with demons that they had vanquished. It would be the Berserkers who would be the shock troops of the Great Mongol who would open up the war and open up the land. The job of the Berserkers was to terrorize the land. They were simply there to inspire fear in others. And that they did. They were the origin of the word berserk and further inspiration for nightmares.

The Vikings Horde sat poised for the invasion and conquest of Aztalan and all of Anahuac. In their numbers and power their confidence grew. Their disdain for "the people" of Anahuac also grew in its intensity. They had determined to wage war on the unsuitable inhabitants of the Promised Land. The longboats were made ready. The Vikings were ready and poised for attacked. Until that time they would eat meat, drink Mead, sharpen their blades, and sing blood-curdling songs.

Chapter 6

A great fire was lighted and the Counsel of Anahuac was convened around it. "The people" were gathering to decide whether or not the join the Mongol Confederation. This would be of the rarest of occasions when Batachikan, a foreigner, would speak before "the people". Batachikan had decided at this point that it was best to avoid a war. He knew that an extended campaign conducted in such a vast country might become a burden to the Empire.

"The Great Mongol comes to you in peace. I bring greetings from the Great Khan. He wishes bountifulness on each of you and your families," opened Batachikan. "It is his wish that your great nation will join with us in a union of peace and prosperity that will be beneficial to us all."

"The people" listened to the words of Batachikan. Hiamovi, Nosh, Tidasi, Heluska, Hiawatha and the rest of the representatives of "the people" studied the measure of his words carefully. Though Batachikan wanted to avoid a war that would tax the Great Mongol he was still a Mongol. He served at the discretion of the Great Khan. He understood that each word which he uttered was an undertaking in the art of war.

He as the closest adviser to the Great Khan had been instrumental in the development of the tactics by which war was waged. It was Batachikan who had come up with the strategies which had led to the safety and not ruin of the Mongol Empire. He had helped develop the countless laws which were weaved into the structure of the Mongol society. Which bound the destinies of all under the Great Mongol to the Great Khan. They would follow the Great Khan anywhere regardless of their own lives.

Batachikan stood as the embodiment of the Great Mongol. He stood before "the people" as an example and intention of what they were to become. He also knew that all warfare was based on deception. To the Northern Horde there was no difference between a lie and the truth.

"We seek only peace with Anahuac," he said while his people were preparing for war. "We seek only trade with you," he said while the Golden Horde amassed at the doorways of Anahuac. "We will usher in a new era of peace and prosperity," he said while his armies of both the east and the west prepared to attack. "We come in peace," he said pretending to be weak while the strongest army on Earth was waiting in the wings. "Our intention is far away from confrontation."

"The people" felt secure at hearing the diplomatic words of Batachikan. He appeared to be an evolved man from the north. Perhaps "the people" could open negotiations with the Mongols. Tidasi studied Naran and Saran as Batachikan spoke. He saw in their expressions the hatred of diplomacy that they tried to cover. Even in silence their faces could not hide their intentions.

"This wonderful nation can do nothing but bring glory to us by your contribution to the Mongol Confederacy. It is the highest honor to be invited to join us. This alliance will provide for your security. Your goods will be traded to all parts of the world without fear from attacks by pirates and will be protected by our law. Your merchant fleet will fly under the banner of our protection and none will dare to circumvent your freedom on the high seas."

Batachikan was the highest mind of the Great Mongol. He was the skillful general who would subdue the enemy without any fighting. He wanted to take Aztalan and Cahokia intact without causing the slightest injury. He wanted to win the war without losing a single man from either side in battle. It was Batachikan who was the inner reason of the Mongol Empire.

"The people" listened to the general of the Great Khan speak to them. They heard the words and inflections in his words. They listened to the meaning of his words, they observed the expressions in his face as he spoke, and heard the intonement of the sounds

Whispers of a Man 69

in his words. They knew that every spoken word was a sound that reverberated and an echo that was carried on the ethers.

"The Great Khan has asked that you will join with us in a peace that will last a thousand years. We have many things which can be given in an exchange of knowledge. I have traveled throughout your land offering the hand of friendship. I can give you the assurance of the Great Khan that your nation we not be changed in any way. I ask that you to consider my words very carefully this day. I ask you to vote with your minds and not with your feelings. We are moving into a new age now. A new world order. Together we will form one government for the entire world. Cahokia will capital of the Great Mongol in the west."

"The people" were silent once Batachikan had finished delivering his address. Then there was some stirring among them. They began to discuss among themselves what they had been told them. The murmuring grew louder.

Hiamovi stood before "the people". There was silence as they sat silently in anticipation of his words. He stood reverently before them collecting the thoughts that he would speak. He looked upon the faces of his family, friends, and delegates who had gathered.

"Peace and blessings of the Great Spirit upon all of us. And peace unto our visitors from the Mongol Confederacy. We welcome visitors from all over the world. Our home has always been open to guests. We welcome trade and exchange, and it has been this way for a more than a thousand years. We are the descendants of the Olmec who first came to this land at the breakup of 'the people' into many tongues long ago. Our ancestors built the pyramids and monuments that we all revere this day. We are an ancient people."

"The people" looked upon the face of Hiamovi and listened to the words that he spoke. Silence filled the place left by the absence of words. There was only one who was speaking among the many thousands of people gathered and that was Hiamovi.

"The beacons of light which burn today are few. Cush and Egypt are threatened, India is fallen, and China is fallen. It is from us that the most perfect union of man and environment has taken place. We have brought the descendants of man from all over the world to live under the most perfect of governments. It is by our law that every man is free and there is no oppression. We are not burdened by taxes and fines though there are many of us. This is because we do not take more than we need. We do not hoard the resources of the Earth. We give respect to other species and honor all life. We do not kill indiscriminately. We are 'the people' of peace," said Hiamovi.

"Today we can feel a hot breath approaching from a far distance. From a world apart an influence comes to us. We are asked to join with a mighty power as friends. We are told that our way of life will improve, and that we will prosper in this new friendship," he continued.

"We are the first nation of the Earth which is still completely intact. All the other first nations have past, or perished, or have been usurped. We are the last of our kind. We are the last of the original man. We have always accepted outsiders to live among us and the blood of many nations now flows among us. It is in harmony that we live according to the law which promotes unity and not discord. The Great Spirit has given us our law and our teacher, Tehuti. Under this law and guidance we are prospering. The law and commandments that we have been given have not failed us," said Hiamovi.

"Change is the way of all things. Our nation is old and the first of firsts. Today we can say that we now live at the highest level of all the nations of the world today. We are the most technologically advance nation on Earth. Do we have the right to expect others to follow our way? Should we follow theirs? Or should we live and let live. This is the question before us this day," Hiamovi continued.

There was silence as Hiamovi spoke. He knew that "the people" understood the meaning of his words. They knew that change was the way of all things. They also knew that they were in line of the first man. Their nation had been established from the line of the first tens kings of the Earth. This was the real reason why the Mongols wanted to take the entire nation intact. It was "the people" themselves who were the treasure.

The Mongols wanted the treasure that was Aztalan because it would validate their existence. To have the descendants from the line of "Zep Tepi" accept them as equal meant that they would receive that which they had been denied before. It was long ago that man had exiled mankind to the Northern Void and built walls around

Whispers of a Man

what was to become Europe. The Mongols were the descendants of the rejected ones. They wanted the acceptance of the first nation of civilization.

"We set the example for mankind to follow. Will we accept that which is lesser as compare to that which is greater? It is not through arrogance that we exist but in adherence to the law of the One."

Hiamovi then became silent. Hiawatha stood before "the people" to speak. Hiamovi was the wisdom of "the people", but Hiawatha was the spirit.

"Peace unto you," he opened. "When the Jaguar first came to this land in the form of the Olmec we kept to the truth and the spirit of the law. It was all the other nations who had lost. We were the only one to keep our original tongue. And to this day we speak the language of Zep Tepi. Throughout time we have adhered to the law. We know that it was the forgetting of the law that brought ruin upon man in the past. Man chose to follow after gods which he knew nothing of instead of following the law and commandment that were set in place for him to follow," said Hiawatha.

"Many from all over the world have visited us with their religions and ideas. And we have been accepting of their visions. It is because we adhere to the Law of the One that we are not corrupted. We can accept differences in religions and outlooks, and we build no places of worship. The Great Spirit of the Universe did not give us religion, but gave us the law," he continued.

"Before we embark on a path that will most certainly change the face of our nation forever we should study the nature of the change that will take place. If Aztalan were to no longer exist then a void would opened in the fabric of reason. And change would be instituted only for the sake of change. Our way is the way of Zep Tepi, Tehuti, and the Olmec. They have not lived in vain," Hiawatha said.

"A mighty nation has come to us asking for friendship. We accept the friendship of that nation. A mighty nation has come to us asking that we join their confederation in a union. We are the creators of the first confederation which still stands. We are asked to understand that acquiescence is the proper course for us," Hiawatha said teaching.

"Listen to my words. This is the wisdom by which we have survived a thousand years and more. We are being asked to understand. In reality, we are asked to stand under. It of vital importance to realize this point. We are asked to understand submission and stand under that which would stand over us. It is we who must overstand. When given a choice be between understanding and overstanding it important to overstand. To stand over means to have knowledge of the past and wisdom to guide us into the future. The choice is such, if you will but know the difference. Will you stand under or over?" Hiawatha finished speaking.

"The people" became silent. Tidasi then stood up before "the people" to speak. He had traveled and seen what had become of "the people" of had resisted the Mongols. He knew that to refuse to become a part of the Great Mongol was to become an enemy of the Great Mongol. He knew that there would be no middle way. He knew that the offer made by the Mongols was not an offer that could be refused without consequences.

"Peace," Tidasi spoke. "We are 'the people' of peace. The wind of change is upon us. We can see what has become of those who have gone before us. We are given two choices. One is the way of the anvil, and the other is the way of the hammer. It is our choice to be made," he continued.

"The choice is ours to decide. Now is the time to decide. If we are to be a people who can be likened to a hammer then we will continue in strength. We will be the master of our own destinies and the captains of our own fates. This is what it meant to be a hammer. If on the other hand if we choose to be anvils then we will live in fear and inevitable disgrace. That which is most important to us will be lost and that is freedom. We will allow everything that we know to be blown away by the winds of change. And we will accept defeat without a fight. We can then be counted as losers without putting up a struggle or fighting for what we believe in," Tidasi spoke stirring "the people".

"Our ancestors, the Olmec, gave their lives so that we might exist to today. They did not put a contingency or a condition on us to fulfill in order to be their descendants. They left us with the law and the criterion. What has made our land and our nation sacred are 'the people'. We are the treasure trove of man. We are the last of the

Whispers of a Man 73

lights which must not be extinguished. We are the burning light of the world wish must not be allowed to go out," he went on. "I ask you to vote not for something that is lesser and not greater. I ask you to vote for our nation and accept the consequences of our decision as men and women of the first civilization. As the Olmec stood against the rebellious Maya we must stand together against tyranny and oppression. If we vote to accept the annexation of our nation then we will cease to exist as a nation. This is the day to stand together and make a decision that stands as our testament for the generations to come that we have gone before them. We are now the ones who will go before the others and they will see what we has become of us," said Tidasi

"The people" listened to Tidasi. Hiamovi and Batachikan listen to the words of Tidasi. Tidasi stood as the well spring of strength. His essence found its source in the bubbling well of the Great Spirit. He was the antithesis of the Mongol. Batachikan saw in Tidasi the primal virtue of a warrior.

Soon Nosh, Heluska, Enapay, Cheveyo, and Kitchi all stood alongside Tidasi before "the people". Then all the other men stood in unison. They stood up for Anahuac. They stood together for Aztalan. They stood tall for Cahokia.

Tallulah was the first women to stand. She stood with her children and with her husband. Then the rest of the women stood and their children also. All "the people" of Cahokia and Aztalan were standing together and not vacillating. They were not going to attract to fear. They could not be frightened by the boogie man of the Northern Void. "The people" of Cahokia were a noble people and there could be no choice between freedom and anything else.

Batachikan sat silently as "the people" made their choice in the matter. Unanimously, did they agree on their collective fates. They chose autonomy and self-rule. He knew that the course and direction of their world was being made with this decision. Naran and Saran smiled their sinister smiles as they knew that this decision would lead to war. This excursion had long ago tried their patience. They like the Vikings longed for the taste of blood.

Batachikan felt disappointment not because he had not been able to bring Aztalan into the Mongol Confederacy but because he would not be able to take the nation intact without bloodshed. He was fully aware that the beauty of Cahokia was its people. If the there was no population then the reward would be half. With no population then the Great Khan would have to administer a vast empty nation. This would be the ruination of the nation. This would be the most undesirable of outcomes.

"'The people' have spoken unanimously," said Hiamovi to Batachikan.

"The Great Khan will be most disappointed. I ask you to make 'the people' understand that it is not the way of the Great Khan accept rejection. Especially when we offer you what we have offered no other nation. We have offered you the opportunity to be the capital of Great Mongol of the west. There is no greater honor or respect that we can offer," said Batachikan to the Hiamovi.

"You have given us a choice that none of us could accept. You offer us an opportunity to accept submission to you, while we are free now. We have no masters above us. We serve only the Great Spirit. You offer us only implied threat of invasion," said Hiamovi.

"We offer friendship," countered Batachikan.

"You offer to opportunity to bow down to you."

"We are offering an alliance."

"We know that you have massed armies to our east and our west," Hiamovi revealed.

Batachikan was taken aback by the revelation of this knowledge. What could he say?

"Yes, we are aware of your intentions. And you say that you offer friendship," Tidasi spoke.

"Yes, I am your friend. I am trying to help you by offering an opportunity to save the face of your nation. You are correct. Our troops are staged. They have not entered the precincts of you lands."

"They have been observed conducting reconnaissance throughout the north of Aztalan. This is not the behavior of friends," Hiamovi said.

"Ku Tu Hiamovi, I am your friend," said Batachikan. "I am here to make peace and offer you whatever it is that you need to show you that we are sincere in our intentions."

"Then pull your soldiers off of the doorsteps to our lands. Ex-

Whispers of a Man 75

change ambassadors and engaged in trade as friends. This gesture would entrust you to us. This would be a show of friendship," said Hiamovi.

"You are wise Hiamovi. I ask you to also be knowledgeable. For as wisdom is of the future it is for a certainty that knowledge is of the past. You are the last of your kind. The Mongol Confederacy does not wish your end. To the contrary we want to help ensure that Cahokia will continue for a thousand years. We know that you are the descendants of the original man. And as you know we are also the descendants of the original man. You great teacher, Tehuti, is also our great teacher, Odin. We do not want to harm you," pleaded Batachikan. "Join with us and make a better world."

Hiamovi, Nosh, Tidasi, and the others listened to Batachikan. They could hear no deception in his words at this time. He seemed sincere in his words. Perhaps he truly wanted to avoid a war. He wanted his people to be allowed to join the ranks of the civilized. Batachikan was truly taken with "the people". He had come to admire the way of righteousness. He could find no fault or reason to despise them.

He could not, however, appear to be weak. Naran and Saran would not allow the emissary of the Great Khan to disgrace him. Batachikan was allowed to acquiesce in order to deceive. He could not grovel at the feet of a people who were clearly seen as a remnant of the pass.

The next day all was silent, but somehow there was a heavy weight over Cahokia. "The people" began to carry a burden. They discussed the proceedings of the night before. "The people" stood en masse to see the visitors from the Great Mongol off as they departed. Batachikan, Naran, and Saran mounted their horses and were provided with food for the long journey ahead. Tidasi, Nosh, Heluska, and Hiawatha escorted the guest to the borders of the lands with Missouri.

Batachikan and his guard sat facing the setting sun. Hiamovi and Nosh had come to respect Batachikan during this time, and he them. Saran and Naran held only contempt for "the people". They were very happy that negotiations had not turned out so favorably. Neither they nor Tidasi had found any common ground. They knew that this was the end of any cordiality that would exist between them. From now on it would be only enmity.

The Mongols moved westward toward their return to Asia and the heart of the Great Mongol. Batachikan was leaving with a heavy heart. He had come to admire to "the people" very much. They rode passed the many pyramids and cities that dotted the landscape. As far as Batachikan was concerned he had left the castle of dreams and the departure was inauspicious. Naran and Saran vowed to return and exact vengeance against "the people". They had observed that Aztalan was a pacifist nation which had no appetite war.

"They are soft and have no stomach for battle," said Saran.

"They will melt before us as butter before a hot knife," added Naran.

Batachikan listen silently as his guard became enthusiastic about prospect of war. He looked longingly at the land. His mind could not stop thinking of the splendor Cahokia. He was a man of war who had grown to admire "the people" of peace.

"The next time that they see us it will be from the unpeaceful end of my arrow and sword. They will come to beg for the mercy and friendship of the Great Mongol. They can contemplate the great spirit of wrath. I will strike the first blew," said Naran.

Throughout the land of Anahuac the Mongols received the same answers to their invitations to join the Mongol Confederation. "The people" of Anahuac had taken the same decision as "the people" of Aztalan and Cahokia. All of "the people" were untied. It was during times of distress and trepidations that "the people" would stand together for the common cause.

The nations of the Yamasee, Washitaw, Missouri, Omaha, Mengwe, Makkah, California, Tslagiwe, Ojibwa, and the others each took their turns to vote in opposition to joining the Mongol Confederacy. The word and results of prior voting had reached each nation before the Mongol delegates had arrived. The wave of Mongol rejection was rippling across the country faster than the Mongols could cross it.

There was not a single vote of dissension to the unanimous vote of the "the people". The Mongols were returning home empty handed and insulted at the outright rejection. This was seen as contentiousness by Naran and Saran. Batachikan still believed that diplomacy was a possibility. He, however, would not speak of this matter to any except to the Great Khan.

The remainder of the journey Batachikan spoke little. Naran and Saran spoke often of war and of being rejected by "the people". They now only wanted show "the people" what it meant to be the enemy of the Mongols.

"You will sit on the throne of the Hiamovi as the Ku Tu of the Great Khan," Saran said to Batachikan.

"Those snakes will bow to our feet," added Naran.

"Mine is to do the will of the Great Khan," said Batachikan.

They traveled back to Asia by one of the Viking ships that had been moored in Vinland. The Mongol and Viking detachments were in complete occupation of the island. The entire island had been transformed within such a short time into a Mongol stronghold. The indigenous people of the island had been enslaved.

Many days were passed on the ship then many more traveling on land before they reach the homeland of the Great Mongol. The Mongol capital of Karakorum came into view from a distance. Karakorum was a large city that spread out over a great distance. The Mongol had positioned themselves at the steeps of Asia where they could deploy strategically to any point. They had adapted to the principle of following the path of least resistance. They were like water. They would suddenly appear and then suddenly disappear. It was from this tactical perspective that they came to occupy more than forty percent of total area of the Earth. They had successfully united the tribes of the Northern Void.

The Northern Void was the incubator of possession and dominance. The Mongols had no code of ethics for the weak or the comfortable. They saw that they were the strong and all others were weak and inferior. They saw the civilized as especially weak. They saw themselves as the wrath of God sent upon the civilized who had strayed from the path. They saw themselves as divinely set loose upon the world.

The Mongol capital city was a bustling metropolis complete with infrastructure and government. It was designed with Babylonian, Indian, and Cushite architecture. They had developed one of the best communications and postal systems in the world. The "Yam" postal system was more efficient than the pony express of the American old west. There were more than twenty thousand schools in the Mongol school system. It was also a policy of the government that its people should be educated and literate.

The Mongols had developed a centralized banking and monetary system complete with paper money which was back by gold, silver, copper, and silk. Trade throughout the empire was conducted along the Silk Road. The Mongols were also extremely tolerant of the various religions. It was the official policy of the government to allow religious freedom.

It was at some point after two thousands BC that the Northern Horde began its descent into civilization. This was begun when the Caucasians began the displacement of the aboriginal and proto-people from the northern lands. The first southern incursion had taken place when the when Northern tribes moved to Iran. Iran took its name from the original meaning "Land of the Aryans". The displacement of the proto-people was not difficult for the Northern Horde because the proto-people of that region had long ago fallen into lethargy. Civilization had become a weak shadow of itself. The condition that the Horde found themselves was one of environmental hardiness that no others possessed.

Slavery was a common practice of the Mongols. Any people who were invaded were summarily put under yoke. During the reign of the Mongols hundreds of millions of people were put to death or enslaved. For "the people" of the world there were two choices and that was accepting invasion or be destroyed.

Batachikan prostrated himself before the Great Khan. He was the closest companion to the Great Khan but even he must follow the protocol and etiquette that all others did when the court was in session. The Great Khan sat high on his throne above all others. He was the direct descendant of the blue-gray wolf and the red-brown deer. No one in his court could sit at or above the same line that he did. The Great Khan sat higher than all under heaven.

"My Lord, you are the most perfect ruler," said the prostrated Batachikan.

"What news of Turtle Island do you bring for me, Batachikan?" asked the Great Khan.

Whispers of a Man

"I return from Anahuac with the answer of 'the people'."
"Speak."
"They were unanimous in their rejection of our proposal."
The Great Khan studied the words of Batachikan considerably before he spoke. He gave Batachikan a long glance. He knew that Batachikan would have done his bidding without hesitation.

"So they are obstinate," the Great Khan replied.

"Yes, your Highness. They have not agreed to join the Great Mongol. They will accept invitation to trade, but they will not acquiesce to us and fly our banner above their's."

The nations of civilization had for the most part always rejected the Mongol ultimatum out of hand. The wheels of war were turning in perpetual motion throughout the Mongol Empire. There was in fact a world war taking place at the time. The Mongols although outnumbered worldwide were on the offensive. They were expanding their territory exponentially. They were fighting simultaneous wars in Asia and Africa. Now they were preparing to enter in to conflict in Anahuac. The Mongol way was the way of the aggressive.

"Did you make them fully aware of the consequences of resistance?" asked the Great Khan.

"Yes, Lord," answered Batachikan.

"Prepare the army and navy to move onto Aztalan."

"Your Majesty, there is a chance that we will be over extended. There is the possibility that all of our wars will tax our treasury beyond capacity," reasoned Batachikan.

The Mongols were equitable when it came to the policy of taxation. Religious organizations and the poor were exempt from taxes. The prisoners taken in war were converted into soldiers of the Great Mongol. The Mongols Empire was built upon the brows and toil of others.

"Our destiny is manifest. We are the wrath of God sent upon the world. It is they who have turned their backs on the Law of the One," said the Great Khan. "We are the manifestation of the brutal truth. We are the truth which the world must accept whether they want or no."

The Great Khan was fully aware of the history and origins of mankind. He knew that the Mongols and Vikings were the hate that hate had created. He also knew his ancestors had been of those who were cast out of civilization so many centuries before. They had been abandoned by the progenitors of civilization to the Northern Void and forgotten. Like the dead rising from the grave they rose from black death to become the ultimate test.

Vikings and Mongols were locked behind the walls that man had built to keep them out. The story went back to the first invaders, the Scythians, Gogites, who rode roughshod around nineteen hundred BC. The barbarians terrorized the civilized world in an all consuming advance. Horde after Horde had swept in from the north like a swarm of locust into the plains of the south.

They were countless and irresistible finding the land before them was like a garden and leaving behind a howling wilderness. None was spared under the battle-ax, not woman or child. The inhabitants of those lands were ruthlessly murdered by the Horde, or if they were fortunate they would be enslaved. Gog would consume all crops leaving herds swept away or destroyed, and the villages burned. All before them was made a scene of desolation. The combined tribes and people of the Northern Void were Gog and Magog. It was from these that the Mongols descend.

"Prepare to move on Anahuac," the Great Khan gave the command.

"It is done, Great Khan," Batachikan said.

"The army will attack by the side door. The Vikings will begin the assault. We will let Aztalan realize what shear violence and aggression can taste like. We fill their bellies with a foul and bitter taste. We shall put constant fear into their minds. They will not rest from the torment that we shall inflict. Like a swarm we shall overwhelm them. Then we shall put the men to death and enslave the women and children," said the Great Khan. "Then shall they beg us for mercy."

"The Great Khan is very wise. They shall come to understand that we are their only friends. The only hope for the world is the Great Mongol. We are the light of the world," said Batachikan. "All under heaven bow to the Great Khan."

The Kurultal, the Mongol senate, convened court to be told of the decision of the Great Khan. Absolute power belonged to the

Whispers of a Man

Great Khan. He had power over life and death. It was the duty of the Kurultal to administer the decision of the Great Khan and not to approve it.

The members who were appointed by the Great Khan were also his most trusted companions who had ridden alongside of him. He had come from among them. He had endured all that they had. He was the most determined of all the Mongols. He was the epitome of their dreams.

Allotments were made for the administration of the campaign. Batachikan would lead the Great Khan's army in to Anahuac. He would be the general of both the army and navy. The Vikings would be under his command and loosely under his control.

The soldiers were given their orders. The war machine was set in motion. Out of the night that covered them they went forth. Like a plague sent was to be the descent of the Northern Horde. They would come by both the lands and the seas. They would suddenly appear and then suddenly disappear. The Mongols believed that it was their destiny to be where they were. And there was no force in the world that could resist them.

"We will attack by the three doors. The Mongol Horde will attack the western flank, the Golden Horde will attack in the east, and the Berserkers will descendant upon them from the top of the world. We will squeeze them in a vise and then chop off their heads," Batachikan planned the assault with Leif.

"I will personally lead the Berserkers to victory," said Leif.

"We will destroy them before you reach the Mississippi. There will be nothing left for you," Leif spoke of glorious victory. "Our banner will fly over their capital within one month of our attack. We will race your men to Cahokia. We will have ravaged their women and children. Nothing will be left for you."

Leif spasmed in his mirth at the hysterical idea that "the people" could put up the least bit of resistant to the might of the Horde. Leif was no philosopher. He was a pragmatist. He only intended to split the skull of Cahokia then chop off its head. He would let the philosophers rebuild it. This was the way of the Viking.

Batachikan was also confident. However, he still believed the "the people" could be negotiated with. He was sure that once Hiamovi saw the might of the combined Northern Horde he would want to avoid war at all cost. Why would they want to risk the destruction of an entire civilization?

Anahuac was far more than an empty space fill with a few large cities. Aztalan and Anahuac contained thousands of cities and towns. It was replete with complete infrastructure which was more advance technologically that of the Mongol Confederacy. Batachikan still believed that Anahuac could be taken intact.

He sat alone contemplating the undertaking that he was about to begin. Silently he sat listening to his own heartbeat. In his silence he thought that he heard a gentle sound carried by the winds. He listened to a sweet sound that played in his mind. Batachikan sat not thinking but listening to the wind. He thought for the slightest moment that heard the sound of a flute.

That night sleep did not come to him. He only sat listening. He knew that war was never as clean and quick as Leif would suggest that it might be. He knew that "the people" although not warlike were not ineffectual. This was the mistake that he felt that the Great Khan and the Vikings were making. Batachikan knew that a land as large and as populated as Anahuac could become galvanized and motivated. He was aware they the Mongols might be waking up a sleeping giant. He as general of the Mongol army and navy must consider all contingencies.

"We will attack in the coldest of winter," Batachikan told his commanders.

The Mongols always opened a war in the winter whenever possible. They would be at an advantage because they had been born in the snow and ice. It was the dead cold of winter when men would shiver before the Mongols and Vikings would cut the limbs from their bodies.

Chapter 7

The counsel chamber light was permanently lighted and "the people" sat knowing that change had come. They also heard the whispers on the winds. They knew that the time had come for a change in them. Time had caught up with them. They also knew that they could not escape the inevitable. And the inevitable was that all things change and nothing remains the same. The young becomes the old. They also knew that the fall would turn to winter. They knew that the Mongols would come.

"Winter is approaching Ku Tu," said Nosh to Hiamovi.

"They will come," Hiamovi replied, "We must prepare now. If we wait it will disastrous for "the people". We will have to build an army quickly and so will the other nations of Anahuac."

"We must make weapons," Nosh said, "Iron weapons."

Anahuac was one of the richest and most fertile lands in the world. It was abundant in mineral resources and raw materials. It had always been known that Aztalan held a great abundance of iron ore. They knew to defend their country they would have to make iron weapons of war.

Fires began to burn all across Anahuac. There was a new enterprise taking place. "The people" had begun to ignite the furnaces of an industrial complex. There were irons works being opened all across the land. The iron making complex was intentionally decentralized and spread throughout the country. Anahuac held vast deposits of iron ore in addition to the other minerals that where abundant in the land.

The metallurgist of Aztalan had been well aware of the richness of the mineral deposits of the land, however, copper was favored over iron because of its beauty. The weapons of the time were made of copper. Weapons were ornamental and iron was not necessary because there was no war. The war machine was put in motion.

Thousands of blast furnaces were built and maintained without end. The eastern wilderness of the Allegheny Mountains held the richest deposits of coal in the world. There was enough coal to keep the fires going for hundreds of years if necessary. It was simple matter to convert the metal works from copper to iron. The iron ore veins were located in many cases adjacent to the already operating copper mines.

The "the people" also built many new mines. Mica was also plentiful in the land and was used an insulator to help maintain the high temperatures needed to cause the reactions for iron production. Mica was also the insulator that was used inside the power generating Great Pyramid of Cahokia.

The coke iron ore was mixed with the limestone and combined with an oxygenation process to produce a type of iron that was more like steel than pig iron. "The people" began weapons manufacture in earnest.

The soon an entire industry began to develop around weapons manufacturing. Metallurgist turned their talents to understanding the design of the projectiles. They began to design blades for various purposes and of designs as well. All the men began to carry long knives made from the new steel.

The arts of swordsmanship and martial war came be to be practiced among "the people". They began to turn their thoughts to more defensive pursuits. Hiamovi appointed Tidasi amir of the new standing army that was to be raised. Heluska was also appointed lieutenant amir. Enapay was assigned position of captain at the head of the large numbers of volunteers that came forth to join with "the people" who would be the first to form the new army. Thousands upon thousands came forth to volunteer. "The people" were in complete accord as their heart brought them to Cahokia to assemble.

"The hearts of 'the people' are starting to beat faster," said Nosh.

"They are beginning to awaken to the prospects of war," answered Hiamovi.

"They do not want war," said Nosh.

"None of us do."

"We have tried to maintain a way of life that has existed since the Olmec. This is a new time now," said Tidasi. "They waited too long to respond to the Mayan threat."

"The people" had come to see Tidasi as embodiment of wisdom, sincerity, benevolence, courage, and strength. He was loved but not feared as was Batachikan. He had been the captain in the Olmec merchant marines. He knew that he would have learned the art of war quickly. He knew that he needed the virtues of a general if he were going to be an effective leader. There was more to being a military leader than reputation.

"Tidasi, here we are," Heluska said to his friend.

"Yes, brother, here we are."

"We must train the first army that Aztalan has seen in hundreds of years. None of us know war."

"You are right. The Mongols are powerful like the giant buffalo," said Tidasi.

"Our people don't know killing," said Heluska, "We will have to awaken something that we do not savor. We must learn to savor the taste of the blood of our enemy. We must learn to kill."

"Killing, this will come with war. I have seen the result of war in other places," said Tidasi. "We must learn to make 'the people' the fiercest of warriors. We must make the enemy dislike the taste of battle with us. How do you hunt the giant buffalo?"

"You divide their ranks until there is only one alone," said Heluska.

"We will make them fight for their lives against an unseen enemy." Tidasi began to lay out the tactic of the army of "the people". He structured his offense as a swarm of hornets. He would structure his defense as an ever changing mist.

Tidasi and Heluska began to make the calculations many times putting together the strategy and battle tactics that would be employed. The first thing that they would do would be to protect the borders of lands. They began building a series of forts resembling castles throughout the land along the water ways. Hundreds of war parties would be sent forth to fortify the doorways of Anahuac. The Olmec merchant marines set up a blockade at the entrance to the

Gulf of Anahuac.

New canals were dug out and existing ones were re-dug. It was here that "the people" were at an advantage. Their intimate knowledge of their own waterways would provide them with a tactical advantage over the Vikings. And their canoes would be more maneuverable than the Viking longboats. The men of Aztalan would not be outclassed in seamanship.

It was on land that "the people" would come under duress. They were far from the caliber of soldier and horsemen that the Mongols and Vikings were. They realize that no matter how much they trained they would never defeat the Horde at their own game. In tactics Batachikan was without equal.

"If we wait for them to attack they surely will," said Tidasi.

"You are right it could be short war," said Heluska.

"We must secure ourselves, but we must also attack," said Tidasi.

It was the prospect of attacking the Mongols that gave Tidasi and Heluska cause to recalculate their conclusions over again. They knew that attacking would be a show of strength. This Tidasi perceived would be a most important tactic.

"No matter how much we prepare against them it will not be easy," Tidasi stated.

"The people will prepare. The problem is the difficulty," said Heluska.

"It will be any mistakes that we make that will give them opportunities. We have to make our blade as feared as the Mongol sword," Tidasi said, while placing one of the new steel long knives and a war tomahawk on the table in front of them. "This will be the difference between life and death. Each of us will learn the way of the blade. Each warrior will carry the soul of 'the people' into battle."

Tidasi would have to come up with "the plan". He would have to out Mongol the Mongols. Yet, he knew that the great difference that existed between the armies was experience. The Mongols were seasoned warriors with hundreds of years of battle tested experience. Tidasi knew that any confrontation with the Mongols Horde could be disastrous to his army, and he knew that the entire army could be destroyed in one battle if they were not diligent in planning tactics.

"We must be able to withstand their initial attack. They will try to route us," Tidasi continued. "We must be able to absorb the initial thrust of their assault."

Tidasi, Hiamovi, and the others knew there would be many lives lost. They also knew there would be no alternative to war. They could sense that everything was going to change. And they knew there was nothing that they could do about it.

"We prepared to die for our home," said one of the warriors aloud.

"We must engage them in a very long campaign," said Tidasi.

"This war will be bad for everyone," said Nosh.

"It will destroy our country," Enapay said.

"We will rebuild," said Hiamovi.

Tidasi and Heluska did not add to the comment of Hiamovi. They knew that the Mongols would never stop and the only recourse would be to stop them. He also knew that his army would have an advantage in knowing the land and terrain. Tidasi knew that the Mongols and Vikings would at first try to take away any options for "the people" to maintain an industrial complex.

Therefore, stock piles of weapons and food would be essential. The knowledge of the natural defiles was also imperative in planning the strategies to fight the incursions. It was logistics that was of necessity in planning of war.

"The people" worked with a sense of urgency as winter approached. "The people" began to build mounds at strategic locations throughout the land. These mounds would serve various purposes. Some would hold stock piles of food and some would hold weapons. Thousands of these mounds were strategically placed throughout the country.

"If you give up now you will be broken later," said Tidasi to his men. "If you are going to die then die here instead of groveling for your lives. They will not show you mercy."

Tidasi and Heluska began to push the men and develop them into warriors. There was a playfulness among the men about the seriousness of the circumstances. Tidasi knew that this was an undesirable penchant which must be eliminated.

"Our men are not nearly the caliber of warriors that can defend against the Mongols," pointed out Heluska.

"We must turn them into warriors or the Mongols will do it," said Tidasi.

He drilled them incessantly. They began to complain. He and Heluska knew that Mongols soldiers like Naran and Saran would make short work of them in their weakness. He had seen the tenacity of the Mongols who had been in their midst. He saw in them the instinctive desire to finish what they started and to finish the enemy.

"You complain. Will you complain to the Mongols? They will make you slaves and then kill you," said Tidasi. The men stopped complaining. They all knew that he was telling the truth.

Tidasi knew that the only way that "the people" could prevail against the Horde would be to outdo them in everything. They must be energetic for the duration of the war, and simulated battle could not replace real battle experience. He knew that lives would be lost early, and that he knew that martyrs would be the real trainers of the men.

"Run!" Tidasi order his men. They ran day and night. They carried heavy loads and drill constantly with the newly developed weapons. The Aztalan technologist did their best to replicate the compound bow of the Mongols. However, the men still preferred the lance and atlatl. They trained in the methods of indirect battle tactics. Tidasi knew that it would be necessary to develop new martial systems of fight. Or perhaps he could revise old ones. Tidasi and Heluska would each take individual command of a legion of men. Their legions would serve as the shock troops for army. They would be comprised mostly of those who had gone and returned from the seas. Only those who had seen the world and knew of what had become of those you went before them and would be knowledgeable enough stand before the Mongols Horde and prevail. Tidasi and Heluska stood surveying the army that was prepared to defend "the people".

Tidasi realized that the warriors of "the people" were to a man far stronger than the Mongol soldiers. He also knew as soldiers the Mongols were superior. The advantage that his warriors might hold would be in the application of the knife. The blade was the traditional in its use among "the people". It had become synonymous with justice. Traditionally "the people" had had carried two blades into battle.

The first blade was straight single edged knife, and the second was a double bladed hatchet called a tomahawk. These were the weapons and traditions that would be reawakened. Tidasi knew that the Mongols and Vikings would have to be close enough in a fight for a blade. He revised the old marital techniques known as the pyramid nine techniques which had been the traditional fighting style of the Olmec.

The tradition of the pyramid nine techniques taught that the blades should attack through nine doors and end at the point of the pyramid. The attack would be made with slashes and stabs along the nine points. It was the infinitely devised combinations of these in an endless rhythm that defined the pyramid. The pyramid could be as small or large and changeable as desired at any given instant.

"Cover your throat at all times," Tidasi taught his men. "Hold the blade in your strong side hand at a forty five degree angle and attack along the nine points of the pyramid."

Soon there was the sound of a whirlwind of knives and tomahawks. The warriors the learned to hook with the tomahawk and to finish with knife. Tidasi knew that the only way for the warriors to become proficient with the blade was to spar. The men began to receive many cuts. Soon after they learn to avoid receiving cuts. The sound of the blade and the tomahawk resembled a buzz saw at work. The pyramid nine techniques combined with the expert grappling skills made the warriors formidable. The warriors practiced night and day.

Tidasi divided his command into clusters. Each cluster was composed of two thousand men. The clusters were divided into groups of five hundred men each. Each group was divided into one hundred man war parties, and each war party consisted of twenty teams of five man bimibas. Each of his commanders was given an objective and alternative objectives based on calculations and intelligence. The orders were then in turn given to each leader of a five man bimiba. Each bimiba was sent throughout the land to teach and carry out its assignment.

It was the ultimate strategy of Tidasi to give each bimiba a mission to accomplish in an area. Each area was a part of a region.

The warriors of the bimiba lived in the area where they were deployed. The bimiba was indigenous to the land. Therefore, each bimiba could operate as an undiscoverable entity, and if captured they would not be able to provide information under torture.

"We must make them believe that we are weak and in disorder," said Tidasi.

"That should not be difficult," said Heluska giving Tidasi an amused look.

"This may not be a bad thing if we use it to our advantage. We must draw them into hand to hand combat. We must take away the advantage of their horses. We are no equal of them as horsemen. We must take them off of their mounts and put them on foot. We outnumber them in terms of sheer numbers.

"How?" asked Heluska.

It was becoming clear that the strength of the Mongols Horde might also be their weakness. If the Vikings and the Mongols held "the people" in such disdain it might be a blow to their morale to make the fight last longer than a short time. The longer that the Mongols and Vikings were made to fight this war the more difficult it would be to persist. The key to this strategy was to take away their mobility. The key to that mobility was the Mongol horse.

"We must make them eat their horses. Once they are on foot we are stronger. Their way is based on movements and maneuvering. We will see how much they like moving over this vast country on foot. They will see that it will be difficult for them resupply and communicate over such a great distance."

The clear strategy was that "the people" would isolate the Northern Horde by cutting them off and making their occupation very difficult. "The people" would make them hate that which they loved most, war. They were developing the tactics of an insurgent war.

"We will not engage them directly. Therefore they will not know where to defend," said Tidasi putting the strategy in place.

We must dispatch bimibas to all sectors of the country. There are many reports of the presence of the Vikings in the north. They are preparing to attack. We must know where it is that they intend to begin their assault. We must stop them before they start," said Hiamovi.

Whispers of a Man

"We must not lose control of the reserves of iron, copper, and uranium," said Nosh. "If they take control of these mines then they will not have to rely on being resupplied from Asia." Heluska would command the group of the protecting Cahokia region, and Tidasi would lead his men to the north into the Michigan Valley south of the Northern Sea. This was the location of the mines.

Cheveyo and Kitchi were assigned to the bimiba that was headed by Enapay. They were assigned along with other the bimibas to the cluster defending the northern region under Tidasi. Enapay's bimiba was sent to survey and gather intelligence about the Viking presence in the north of Aztalan.

Enapay's five man bimiba, including his brothers, moved five days journey to a place above at the edge of the Northern Sea in the Great Michigan Valley. There they saw the first evidence of the Viking presence in the land. They observed a flotilla of longboats in the distance ferrying soldiers and materials across the inland sea.

"They are planning to invade from here," said Enapay. This was the first official sighting of the Vikings in the lands. Before this sighting there had been only rumors of their presence.

"There are so many of them," Kitchi said.

"This is the evidence that we have been looking for," replied Enapay. "We must get word back to Tidasi."

"Quiet," Cheveyo said in a low voice. There was a squad coming directly at them. The bimiba had painted their faces and bodies with the colors of nature. They appeared practically invisible to the noisy Viking contingent as it passed by.

"They stink," said Cheveyo.

"Yes," said Enapay.

"They are very loud," said Kitchi.

"It will be no secret when they approach," said Enapay.

The bimiba followed the Viking patrol further until they reached the camp that was made on the shore of the Northern Sea. There was the strong smell of death permeating the air everywhere. Something had died recently.

"The smell is awful. What is it?" asked Kitchi.

"It is the smell of death," said Enapay.

They continued to search for the source of the stench. As they drew nearer to the source of the smell it grew more acrid. They stepped into a thicket to find a horrifying scene. The men were silenced by the shock that they beheld. There were bodies lying about. The victims had been hacked to death by Viking battle-axes and swords.

All the victims had been dismembered and beheaded. Each also had been scalped and their faces torn from their skulls. This was a scene none of the bimiba could have ever imagined.

"How could they?" said Kitchi angrily.

"We must kill them," said Cheveyo as he withdrew his blade from its scabbard.

"Wait," said Enapay, "Now is not the time. We are here to learn of their intentions and actions."

"What of these people?" said Cheveyo, "Who will fight for them?"

"We will fight for them, but now is not the time. We will only die and there will be no justice. We will wait and report what we have seen."

The bimiba placed all the bodies in a pile and covered them with soil. When they had finished there was a burial mound where there had once been carnage. The men made prayers for the dead. The bimiba continued to gather reconnaissance about the Viking present in the north. They could see from the evidence that was brazenly left by the Vikings of their mercilessness. They decided to leave message for the Vikings in return. They stealthily rigged a trap that was used for the purpose taking down the giant short-face bear that sometimes extended its feeding territory to close to populated areas.

Enapay had faced the giant bear during his excursions to the wilderness. He had learned build the fatal trap for the creature, because when facing the giant short-faced bear there were no second chances. The trap had to be very deadly. It was composed of a triggered pendulum equipped with extremely sharp spikes that would impale the body of the beast.

The trap was built, loaded, and locked into place. The bimiba headed back to report to Tidasi the details of its findings. They had not traveled a far distance when they heard the anguished screams of what seemed to be the voices of men. Something terrible had happened. The same party of Vikings that had been seen earlier

Whispers of a Man 93

had walked into the trap. Four of them had been impaled by the vicious spikes of the short-faced bear trap.

Their were continuing screams that were the sounds of anguish that were coming from another of the Viking's who had not been killed instantly by his injury. The Viking had remained impaled and lodged on the trap. The pain that he felt was the sharpest that could be imagined. He hung suspended and impaled by the spikes suffering for what seemed like an eternity and then he died.

The bimiba lead by Enapay did not wait to savor the taste of revenge. They listened at a distance to the sound that was carried to their ears by the winds. It was the sound of a distant roar of the Viking marines. They were lamenting over the bodies of the men who had been killed.

"We must attack now. We must take revenge," said Iggle.

"No, we will wait for the order to attack from Batachikan," rebutted Leif.

"Our men are thirsty for the taste of their blood," replied Iggle.

"I will taste the blood of the first man who disobeys my orders. We will wait until the order to attack is given."

The Vikings did their best to remove the bodies of their dead comrades intact. However, this proved to be very difficult. The limbs of the bodies were ripped from the torsos during the extraction process. The torsos of the dead Vikings had been ripped apart by the spikes of the trap.

The ripped and torn torsos, limbs, and heads of the dead Vikings were placed in a gory pile of flesh, blood, and bone. The pile was then set ablaze. Dark smoke and a sickening stench filled the air. Those present began to choke on the disgusting flavor which they inhaled. Iggle and the Berserkers savored the foul stench and they let loose a bloodcurdling howl that carried down the Mississippi.

"They have amassed in the north at edge of the Northern Sea. They have slaughtered villagers," Enapay reported to the Tidasi.

"They have begun killing," said an incensed Kitchi.

"We must take revenge on them," said Cheveyo.

"What are their numbers?" asked Tidasi.

"There are many thousands of them. As big as the sea. There is an entire army to our north. They will come," replied Enapay.

"Were you able to discern their intentions?"

"There are hundreds of longboats. They will come down the river. They are planning to control the river."

"We cannot let that happen," said Tidasi. "Move your warriors north, Heluska. We cannot wait any longer. War has come. We will blockade the river. We will not let them on the waters."

Heluska's party then began the task of blockading and reinforcing the northern Mississippi basin in Wisconsin. This area was now to become the primary front for the army of "the people". Tidasi and Heluska were well aware it was in the north that vulnerabilities lay. There were no mountains or canyons that acted as natural defenses. The Northern Sea and the Mississippi could become highways to bring the enemy into their midst.

Chapter 8

The Mongol Horde began their descent into the heart of Anahuac by way of the back door. The sound of thunder was the sound made by the hooves of their horses. Thousands of them came pouring out of the Northern Void. This army moved and the sky above them became darken. They consumed all that was in their paths. All animals fled before the fire that was their march. They practiced their marksmanship by killing everything that they saw.

Batachikan moved with his men. This movement was intended to be an expansion into new territories. They were bringing with them the tools and materials for permanent settlement. The Mongols had no intention of ever leaving. One of the men planted the banner in the soil of the land. This was a declaration of their sovereignty.

"Turtle Island is now and forever a part of the Mongol Confederacy," said Batachikan as the soldier planted the banner.

The Mongols had now officially lay claim to the land that was before them. They lay claim to a land that was occupied by millions of inhabitants. They had made their declaration and claimed an entire continent without consideration to those who were living on it. This was a declaration of war.

The Vikings simultaneously began their assault on the eastern wilderness. They began moving across from Greenland. They entered Anahuac from the northeast under the command of banner of Thor. These Vikings were known for the powerfully large and heavy hammers that they wielded.

The Viking army of the east began to secure the eastern coast of Anahuac where they met little resistance. They began enslaving all of those that did not flee. They fashioned a giant iron hammer to place in the ground to announce their presence and to mark their claim to the land. All of Anahuac that lay between the two great oceans was now claimed by the Mongol Confederacy. "The Greatest War" had begun in earnest.

The Navy of the Olmec in the Gulf of Anahuac extended its blockade. The Viking longboats would not be allowed to penetrate and the Mongol Navy could not come within reach. The Northerners were barred from the region. The Olmec Navy would not hesitate to fire upon them with the focused energy beam apparatus that their ships carried.

The Allegheny Mountains would provide a natural barrier and obstacle to the Great Estate in the east, as would the Rocky Mountains in the west. "The people" began to set traps throughout the wilderness. Bimibas were sent into the wilderness to agitate and harass the Vikings. They would make the Vikings weary of the heavy weight of the weapons and armor that they carried through the dense forest.

"The people" set deadly welcomes at every turn. The land became treacherous and dangerous. "The people" began to draw out copper wire and lead plates. They buried them throughout the land in parallel tracts. They place coils of copper intermittently along the highways where the Mongols horses would trek. Periodically a high-energy pulse would be sent into the coils and the Mongols would suddenly find their horse dropping dead from heart attacks.

"We will allow them to enter into Anahuac on horseback. They will leave on foot," said Tidasi.

"The people" now saw the necessity of learning the evils of war. This was also a two-edged sword because they had no experience in war. They would learn by trail and error.

"The longer that we will engage them the duller that their weapons will become," said Heluska.

"We will make them long for home. We will make them hate the thing that they love the most, war," Tidasi continued outlining his plan. "The key will be to cause them delays in executing their plans in everything that they attempt."

Hiamovi and Nosh listened to the battle tactics of Tidasi. They knew that his plan was the hope of "the people". However, it would not only be costly to the Northern Horde, but it would be costly to "the people" as well. Hiamovi knew that Tidasi was the arbiter of "the people's" fate. Tidasi was the man who the nation would depend on to prevail or to perish.

*****

With the sunrise in the east the Mongol horses began their push further south. The recently assembled "The People's" Army of the western nations was there to meet them. The combined nations of the western coastal regions had begun to prepare for invasion upon the occupation of Vancouver Island.

"The People's" Army of the west was composed of different nations moving as a coordinated front to meet the enemy. All of the warriors had been equipped with the new weapons that had been recently developed. The warriors moved northward to meet the Mongols at the first battle of Anahuac. One hundred thousand of them marched forward.

"Tell them to surrender or be destroyed," Batachikan gave the order to his messenger.

The Mongol messenger entered into the midst of "The Peoples" Army of the western nations. The messenger gave but on message, "Kneel or die".

"You tell Batachikan that the Makkah will never allow you to invade our lands, or to move through it," said the amir of the Makkah.

With that the war in the west was begun. That night a single arrow was fired through the air from a great distance. It was shot from a Mongol compound bow. It had been set ablaze so that its path could be followed in the air. The arrow landed in the heart of the camp of "The People's" Army. Upon its landing there was an explosion and roaring blaze was immediately started. The arrow had landed in a cache of supplies stored for the expedition.

The warriors clamored to put out the blaze. Then there was silence. The men waited silently for the attack. It never came. The Mongols tactic had been one of intimidation. That night none of them slept. At the first light they began to move forward to meet the Mongol Horde.

The sun rose in the silence of the beautiful day in the season of winter. The birds appeared particularly agitated this day. The air was crisp and the sky was sunny and blue. It was the beginning of the winter. It was a beautiful day.

There was a sound heard coming from a distance. It was a peculiar sound not unlike the sounds of hornets swarming. The sky became black as a distant cloud approached. The sound turn into the sound of thunder and the black cloud grew ominously closer. Then the sky opened up and it began to rain arrows upon "The People's" Army of the west.

The Mongols Horde had drawn the warriors forward with a single shot and fired tens of thousands of arrows over the heads of the army. Now deadly thunder blots were falling upon them. There were so many arrows falling that it seemed as if it was raining from heaven.

The Mongols reloaded and re-fired again and again. The hail of death seemed that it would never end. There was no place for the warriors to run. Their bodies were riddled with arrows. It seemed that there were hundreds of arrows for each of them. The warriors dropped by the hundreds. Most of those who stood at the front were killed and the remainder had been mortally wounded.

When the rain of arrows stopped, and the sunlight and blue sky filled the air again, and the dark cloud had past only the moans of the dying could be heard in the silence. There were a few men who miraculously had not been killed or wounded. The carnage of the scene of death was unimaginable. Bodies lay in heaps everywhere. The survivors had been lucky enough to have been shielded by the bodies of their fallen brothers.

"Move forward," Batachikan gave the order to move toward the fallen army. Naran and Saran ordered their soldiers to march upon the killing field. The survivors were taken prisoners and brought before Batachikan. The Mongols went as death angels killing each wounded soldier in turn who had not been killed by the rain of arrows.

"Will swear your allegiance to the Great Mongol?" Batachikan asked the warriors who had been brought before him.

"We will never join you. We will die now," said the prisoner.

The Mongols then took each of the men in turn and tied them to four horses by their arms and legs. The order was given and the warriors were drawn in four directions by the horses and ripped into quarters. This scene went on for each of the men until the last remained.

"I will ask you," said Batachikan. "Will you acknowledge Great Mongol as your sovereign?"

"I am Makkah of Anahuac. We will never accept barbarians as our masters," said the last warrior of the Makkah remaining alive at the front.

"We will occupy your lands. We will enslave your women and children. We will destroy everything that you know and love. Your home will be no more. If you acknowledge our sovereignty your people will be spared. It is up you to save your people. Think of them," said Batachikan attempting to reason with the warrior.

"'The people' will fight you forever. When you kill me, as you did my brothers, my spirit will rise to fight you. And others will come to take my place. Hurry and kill me. I seek to rejoin my brothers."

Naran and Saran savored the opportunity for exactitude on the insulin dog who dared not bow down to the Great Mongol. If Batachikan was the thoughtful reason behind the Horde then Naran and Saran was its rage.

"Let us help you rejoin your brothers, then, die dog," said Naran.

"Are you proud?" asked Saran.

"Join your brothers then," said the Sun and the Moon, Naran and Saran, sang out together and laughing hysterically.

The last prisoner was then tied to four horses that were facing in the four directions. The warrior lay looking into the eyes of Batachikan defiantly and smiled in his direction. Batachikan gave the order and the prisoner was drawn and quartered. The Mongols began to dismember the bodies of the remaining dead.

This was witnessed by from a distance by thousands of warriors waiting as reserves in the hills surrounding the valley. This act enraged and incensed the warriors. Each of them became charged. They all rose to counterattack. The act of dismembering their dead brothers helped revived the demoralized army. Each of them forgot about their own lives and became immortal.

Then there was another black cloud appearing in the sky. This time ominous cloud was moving toward the Mongols. The warriors of "the people" had launched their lances simultaneously. It began to rain lances on Mongols.

A roar broke the silence. Like the sound of thousands of roaring jaguars the warriors began to shout. This was a shout that the Mongols had never heard. The horses became nervous. A wave came rolling out of the surrounding hills. Thousands more of the Anahuac warriors came pouring into the valley where the massacre had taken place.

The Mongols were taken by surprise. Their estimates had told them that the warriors of "the people" were not cunning and were of no threat. Before they could assemble their ranks the warriors of Anahuac were close enough to use a blade.

With swords drawn the warriors of the western army of Anahuac descended into the valley. Wave after wave they came. The Mongol arrows once again filled the sky. The warriors wielded their shields for protection. Soon they were close enough for hand to hand combat.

The warriors of "the people" began to cut at the legs of the horses. Each of the incensed warriors fought like ten. They would not yield. Soon the army of Califa, the Queen of California, joined the fight. Her Amazons were poured into the battle sending their own arrows into the midst of the Mongol Horde. The Amazons of Califa were a powerful force in their own right. They were among the most disciplined warriors of "the people" of Anahuac. They had learned long ago to fight with the tenacity and intensity of men.

"You come to conquer, Mongol?" said Califa as she fired arrow after arrow into the heart of the Horde, "Conquer this."

A Mongol solider approached the Queen of California with sword in hand preparing to deliver a killing blow. She was knocked to the ground by the force of his blow. She had not been hurt. She had managed to parry the blow expertly. She turned to face the soldier with her blade in hand. He leaped to pounce on the opportunity to finish the queen. She met his pounce and leap with a thrust of

Whispers of a Man

her blade into the heart of the Mongol. She cut his throat after she removed it from his heart.

The Mongols began to receive heavy casualties. They had been celebrating an early victory. Now they found themselves on the defensive. They turned as if to retreat. This was a favorite tactic of the Mongol Horde. All warfare is based on deception. Then immediately they regrouped with Mongol precision, turned, and began to redirect the energy of the Anahuac warriors. The fighting went on fiercely. Warriors and soldiers fell.

Naran and Saran entered the field of battle killing all those who lie in their path. They wielded their swords like a whirlwind. They mowed down the warriors as they went. A smile highlighted their blood soaked faces. They savored the flavor of the kill.

Batachikan also joined in the battle. He had also been surprised by the counterattack of "the people". From horseback he fired tens of arrows in succession. It was he who was the quintessential soldier. Fighting resistant enemies had been his way of life for many years. He had seen both the strong and the weak of the resistant. To Batachikan it did not matter. He had no compunction about killing enemies of the Great Mongol.

Soon there were tens of thousands of men and women of the army of western Anahuac in armed conflict with the Mongols. The close quarter combat went on all of that day. Death toll reached more than fifty percent of the warrior army of "the people". The death toll of the Amazons of Califa exceeded seventy-five percent. That day all of the twenty nations of the west suffered greatly. The Mongols advance to the south had not been stopped but had been rerouted. It had been delayed, turned, and had given "the people" more time.

"Are there more of you," said Naran as he hacked his way through "the people."

"Where are you going my friend? Come here," said Saran killing another warrior.

More reinforcements from west of the Mississippi began to arrive to sure up the front. Many more mounds began to appear throughout the land. Death, carnage, and mounds where everywhere. The Mongols reinforcements also arrived from the north. The Mongols had suffered heavily this day as well. They also piled their dead. However, they did not bury them, they burned them. Cremation was the way of the Northern Horde.

The Mongols relished in the frenzy of the moment. The warriors of "the people" were defeated and were forced to retreat to the south into the coast of Oregon and California. The Mongols did not pursue "the people" in their retreat. Batachikan knew that it was unwise to pursue a retreating enemy. He let them go.

"General, we have defeated them," said Naran as he plunged his sword into another wounded warrior.

"Have we? How?" answered Batachikan. "We have taken many casualties."

"They are taken five times as many."

"They still come."

"Yes, then we will kill them all."

Batachikan realized that the battle had been won, but victory had not been achieved easily. He also saw the he had made a critical misjudgment. His army had incensed "the people" by mutilating the bodies of the fallen warriors. The warriors had become buttressed by the act of desecration.

Although "the people" had suffered a tremendous defeat they had instilled into the mind of Batachikan that they would fight. He also realized that the Great Mongol would never be accepted. He realized that "the people" had to be conquered. This would mean that Anahuac could not be taken intact.

A significant casualty that Batachikan saw as a vital statistic was the reduction in the total number of Mongol horses. The warriors of "the people" seemed to be targeting the horses. This strategy could provide a mobility problem for the Mongols. They would have to counter this tactic by taking Anahuac horses.

Realizing that this campaign would be a long one it became imperative to take advantage of the local resources and to mix those resources in with that of the Mongols. Batachikan then ordered his soldiers to change tactics. He realized that in such a vast country he must conserved his own resources. He would use his foot soldiers to lure "the people" forward then encircle them with the cavalry and attack.

The army of the west had retreated to the border of Oregon and California. They had suffered significant losses of over half of its warriors in the opening battle of the war. As they reached the border they found volunteers waiting to fill the ranks of the fallen. The army of the west was immediately redoubled.

Cahokia soon heard word of the battle of northwest Anahuac. They had also heard that the army of the west had suffered heavy losses but had not been defeated. In fact, they had also inflicted heavy losses on the Mongols as well.

"The Makkah, California, and the other nations have fought valiantly," said Hiamovi.

"We must send help to them," said Nosh.

"We cannot. This will leave us vulnerable to attack from the north and east. We must hold our positions," said Tidasi.

"What about the west?" asked Nosh.

"The Missouri and the Omaha are en route," answered Heluska.

"They will meet the Mongols as they advance. 'The people' of the northwest know that they must only weaken and hold the Mongols for as long as they can. Reinforcements from Amexum and Kemanahuac will be arriving. This first battle has been fought but the war is far from over," said Tidasi.

"The people" all over the world began to become galvanized. Volunteers from the Cushite nation began to arrive to join in the fight. This was not just an attempt to forestall the invasion of Anahuac. This was going to be a major movement to repulse the Mongol Horde out of Anahuac and all the way back to Asia.

Chapter 9

The news of the invasion of Anahuac reached around the world. The Cushite peoples of the world became galvanize in opposition to the aggression. The nations of Amexum, Africa, began to send reinforcements. The Egyptians also assigned warriors to the fight in Aztalan, and Canaan joined in the fight. The South Kemanahuac nations sent reinforcements as well. The world war to be fought on the soil of Anahuac was building up.

People of African and Cushite descent had always lived in Anahuac and Kemanahuac. They began to arrive during the process of desertification of the Sahara in searching for new lands to live. With the desertification of the lands of the Sahara the lands of the north became more temperate. These new temperate lands became the northern lands of Anahuac. "The people" of the world were coming to the defense of their own.

The Mandinka nation was one of the first to send an armada the take part in the defense of Anahuac. The Mandinka were a prosperous nation from the west of Africa. They had been longtime trading partners with Aztalan. They not only sent hundreds of ships laden with aid but many thousands of warriors as well. Their navy was assigned to defend the Ethiopian Ocean and the entrance to the Gulf of Anahuac.

The invasion of Anahuac was the continuation of the Mongol war that had been raging worldwide and had only now reached Anahuac. The eastern and northern parts of the world had been at war with the Northern Horde for more than a thousand years. This was the final assault of the Northern Horde to subdue the entire

Cushite civilization who they viewed as having rejected them from the beginning.

It was the ultimate realization that this war was fight for world supremacy. This was a war of the north versus the south. This was worldwide civil war. The Northern Horde believed they had been slighted by man by being denied its proper place in the family of nations. And the Cushites were adamant about the barbarians from the north being kept out. This conflict was about ideology. The dark skinned people of the world did not believe the lighter from the north worthy of redemption.

So the armies gathered in their masses. The generals concocted their incantations in the cauldrons of their imaginations like witches at black masses. The minds of all became consumed with the destruction of the other. Each deemed the enslavement of the other a viable alternative to union.

Soon the kingdom of Mali also began sending warriors to participate in the liberation of Anahuac. This expedition was led by the sultan of Mali himself. Upon his departure he left his brother Mansa Musa on the throne of Mali. After a time Mansa Musa sent another contingent to Anahuac. This contingent upon finding the full extent of the war continued up the Mississippi to reinforce Cahokia.

The population of Cahokia grew to more than five times because of the influx of refugees fleeing the invaders and because of the warriors arriving as reinforcements. The face of the Cahokia and Aztalan had already been changed forever. The city and countryside were brimming with new life. The richness of the land still continued to support them.

With the many warriors who arrive on the shores of Anahuac came their religions. The warriors who arrived in the land were maintainers of the Law of the One. Anahuac came to be a land of many peoples and diverse religions. Cahokia absorbed the new people and their religions. The basis was the law.

"Our country is vast. The greater our population the more difficult it will be for them. They will become bogged down by their own weight," said Hiamovi.

"There are many of them. Our country is becoming a killing field. It will be difficult for us to maintain control," said Nosh.

The refugees and warriors quickly integrated themselves into the forces of "the people". Hiamovi devised that integration would be the greatest strategy in keeping the country whole. He realized that all the new inhabits of Cahokia should have a tie to the land. Then "the people" opened the land to all except the Northern Horde. The land was open to all those who obeyed the law of the Great Spirit.

Soon new laws were being instituted. "The people" began to adopt a posture that guaranteed security to the citizens of Cahokia. These laws gave them an advantage. There was a continued influx of "the people" of northeast, the Mengwe. They had coming fleeing before the Vikings. These refugees wanted the same rights as "the people" of Cahokia.

"We must maintain sovereignty of Cahokia," said Matawau, a councilman.

"We cannot oppress our guests," said Nosh.

"This is our land and we must ensure that we are not lost in our own home. There are many foreigners here but this is still Cahokia. Our citizens must maintain the highest class here. Others who are not born here cannot be allowed to share sovereignty with us," stated Matawau.

"Yes, you are correct that this is our land. We have never spoken of this before. We have always welcomed all," said Hiamovi.

"This is a different time now. Things cannot remain as they were. If we do not pass new laws now we will be outnumbered and overrun."

"Perhaps it will be new laws that will cause problems. We have rarely passed any new laws," said Nosh.

Late in the evening as the sunset in the west did all "the people" and the warriors from around the world bowed down to pray together. Once again did the family of man come together to face mankind. Mankind was the face of those who saw to exalt themselves above the law of the One. Mankind was incorrigible.

Mankind was bent on the final destruction of man. Mankind wanted to bring man to his knees under the yoke of the Great Mongol. This was the dilemma in which man found himself. "The people" knew there could be no peace. They knew there could be no compromise.

That evening the counsel chamber light still burned brightly and "the people" began to write new laws. The laws divided "the people". The laws drew distinctions among "the people". The new laws created differences between them. The counsel wrote amendments to the existing laws which guaranteed sovereignty and position to "the people" of Cahokia forever. The Mengwe who were the closest relatives to the "the people" disapproved vehemently of the new laws.

"The Mengwe are our closest of family. Why do we pass these laws?" said Hiawatha. "They will only serve to divide 'the people'. This is how 'the people' will be lost. We will be divided and conquered."

"We are still family. These laws will ensure that all "the people" will maintain their rights," said the council Matawau.

Hiawatha saw the division taking place among "the people". He knew that it was spirit which held "the people" together. "The people" were dividing themselves before the perceived threat. The Mongols had not asked them to make these divisions but the took this upon themselves.

"It is the division based on the law which separates 'the people'. Now we have begun with a thought. This thought is the seed of dissension which is a tiny crack in the fabric of our character. This seed is growing into suspicion and distrust. We will begin the distrust our brothers and will be counted among the lost," said Hiawatha.

"We are insuring the prosperity of Cahokia and of our children. Can we be blamed for protecting our lands?" reasoned Matawau"

"There is no one to blame but ourselves for inviting darkness into our home. The darkness that we invite is the suspicion and guilt that each of will now carry with us. We cannot do injustice to our brothers and not expect retribution. Remember the feather of justice which is the foundation of civilization."

Hiamovi and Nosh listen to the tone that was being spoken. They knew that no good could come from adding any laws that confounded the laws that had been giving in the beginning and had not needed to be changed until now.

"We must be very careful about making many new laws at one time. Now is the time for patience and perseverance. We must respect the freedom that is enjoyed by all of us. If we deny the freedom of any other than we deny our own freedom. The road which we are beginning to travel is a dangerous road. Perhaps we will find ourselves fighting two enemies," said Hiamovi.

The counsel chamber light burned. Hiamovi, Nosh, and Hiawatha argued honorably to resist the temptation to pass any laws which limited the individual freedom of any, including the refugees. Arguments were made and votes were taken. And the new laws were passed. With the passage of the new laws "the people" began to divide themselves.

Chapter 10

The Vikings continued their descent from the north down in to the eastern seaboard of Anahuac. "The people" began a campaign of indirect engagement. War parties consisting of one hundred warriors would strike the Viking Marines and then scatter. This tactic caused great frustration for the Vikings.

"These savages are cowards," said Edgar the Viking commander in the east.

"We'll chase them until they drop," said his lieutenant Ivan.

In their frustration the Viking Marines would chase the warriors. Over and over the Vikings were led into traps. Many times the Vikings were entrapped and brought close enough for a blade. In close quarter combat the Vikings were limited in wielding their large heavy weapons. The Vikings were ill equipped and trained for warfare in the dense forest of the east. Even in the winter "the people" were able to utilize the terrain.

"Those snakes are slithery. Watch yourselves," barked Edgar.

"Ahhh," scream a soldier who had stepped into a hold lined with poisoned tipped spikes. He immediately began foaming at the mouth. The poison attacked his central nervous system like the venom of a snake. His eyes begin to bleed and his heart burst. His comrades stood opened mouth while this horrible death stuck like a hammer. The Viking patrols began to become weary of moving out from their encampments.

"Its not my turn to go on patrol. I just went out," said one of the soldiers who had become wary.

"Up you coward. Do you want to face them or me," snarled

Edgar.

The Vikings in the east turned themselves into an army of occupation. Soon the Celts arrived to reinforce the Viking Marines in the east. The Celts were very powerful soldiers who fought along with the Vikings in hope of gaining a piece of the prize that was Aztalan.

The Welsh under their prince Madog also came in allegiance to the Great Mongol to the join the occupation forces in Anahuac. Together, with the Celts and the Welsh, the Vikings began to build fortresses as they moved. They were powerful fighters who were deployed at the discretion and as a part of the Northern Horde. They entered the shores of Anahuac under the banner of Christianity.

"The people" came to discern that the Vikings and the rest of the Golden Horde were of blond hair, blue eyes, and red beards. This was the first appearance of those descendants of mankind in the Promised Land. This demarcation discerned the difference between man and mankind.

It was a force that was being wrought with the invasion of Anahuac. That was the introduction of Christianity into the land. The Great Mongol had promised those of the new religion freedom and land in return for their participation in the war. Vikings were eager to form an alliance with the Christians. In this strange and hostile land they needed all of the allies they could get. The Celts and the Welsh became enthusiastic soldiers for the cause of the Great Mongol. They were sent to the front to seek and engage the warriors of "the people".

"They run like rabbits," said a Celtic soldier.

"Running for their lives," said another and laughing at the humor of the image of running rabbits.

The Welsh and the Celts found themselves facing little resistance during their advance through the land. However, any and all reconnaissance were brought to the blades of "the people" and never again heard from. The Celts and the Welsh were only allowed to advance in their march through the land and never allowed to retreat. They kept moving forward through land.

"We must save these godforsaken heathens from themselves. We are going to save them even if we have to kill all of them," said Madog to his men.

They began to erect large wooden crosses as markers they traveled throughout the land. They also intended to spread their religion throughout the land. "The people" began to carve hieroglyphic symbols into the bodies and arms of the crosses. The hieroglyphics carved within served as totems telling the stories of the events that were taking place. This was the beginning of the totem pole.

After a while a great number of the Celts and the Welsh were cut off from the Vikings and the Northern Horde and were not heard from again. They would soon come to the realization they were caught in the long trap and there was no way back home.

"Push forward," said Madog.

"They will not fight us in the open," said one the Welsh soldiers, "They hit and run like cowards.

"Push forward," repeated Madog. One by one the Celts and the Welsh were diminished until they became a fraction of their numbers. Soon the Europeans found themselves marooned and isolated and living off the land to survive.

"We must return to the east," said one of the Celts. As he turned to point in the direction of the rising sun his heart was pierced by an arrow. The Welsh and the Celts would not be allowed any regress.

"Push forward," shouted Madog again to his men.

The Vikings wiped out all of "the people" on sparsely populated East Coast of Anahuac who opposed them and enslaved those who had not escaped. The coastal villages became easy prey and were quickly abandoned. "The people" of the east sought the refuge of the mountains of the eastern wilderness, the Allegheny Mountains. Those who were not destroyed fled to the internal security of Aztalan and Cahokia. "The people" of the east maintained constant harassment of the Vikings through forest warfare tactics. The Vikings soon came to despise "the people" and began to call them snakes.

"I hate these snake," said one of the Vikings who carried a large hammer.

"They will not fight like men," said another.

Mutilations began to be commonplace. More and more mounds began to appear throughout the land. Scalping, disfigurement, and dismemberment began to be synonymous with this war. Everything and everyone was affected by grotesqueness that was taking place all around. "The people" also adopted the tactics of mutilations. The land began to be stained red.

"Their spirits will never be at peace," said one of the warriors. "The people" believed that the dead did not rest if their bodies were disfigured at death.

A Viking captive was taken in the eastern wilderness. He was beaten with a sharp throne bush mercilessly and dipped in the burning hot pitch. The Viking marine was then set a blaze where his body soldered for days filling the air with the foulest of stenches. The Vikings grew ever angrier at the victimization of its soldiers.

"The people" began to take on the personification and nature of violence. They were highly incensed by the tactics of mutilations as practiced by the Vikings. As the Viking soldier was mutilated "the people" stood watching in a surreal glee as the tortured victim agonized. "The people" were became as vicious as the Vikings.

The Vikings continued to chase, but the chase never caught up with the ghost. "The people" had become as ghosts to the Vikings. The hunters became the prey as the Vikings were lured into the traps that were set for them. The warriors would suddenly appeared and would suddenly disappear. The Vikings would lie in wait for an enemy that would never appear. They would pursue an enemy they would never catch. And they would fall into more traps.

In the long cold days of the winter's nights the howling of the wolves and the beating drums sang in chorus. The wolfhounds hungrily awaited the feast that was to come. Their fangs drooled with their infected saliva. They hungered for the taste of "the people". The Berserkers were ready to enter the field. Like wild animals to be cut loose from their chains the Berserkers were set loose upon the land.

"Forward," said Leif giving the order to march on mine fields.

"It is about time. We want blood," shouted Iggle. "Forward to the feast."

Dressed in skins of wolves and bears they came out of the northern void like a plague sent from the depths of frozen hell. The giant demons began their deadly march. Taking the lead was Iggle, Erik the Blood Ax, and Forten the Skull Splitter. They beat on their shields with their swords.

Whispers of a Man 115

Leif, Ivar the Bones, and Olaf the Stout led the legion of wolfhounds that would be sent in to devour "the people" who came within biting distance. The Berserkers marched forward to cross a frozen lake that lay in their path.

"Attack," shouted Heluska to the army has he launched his lance through the chest of one of the Berserkers. The Viking clutched the spear in shock as he looked at it protruding from his chest. The Berserkers sang out a bloodcurdling howl.

"Let loose the hounds," shouted Leif.

"Kill them all," shouted Iggle.

The warriors of "the people" began to rain a shower of lances and arrows upon the Berserkers. Many of the giant Vikings fell. Like locomotives the Vikings began their counterattack. They began to pick up speed and power as they gained a full head of steam. The wolfhounds were the first to reach the warriors.

The sound of thunder could be heard rumbling toward the wolfhounds and the Vikings. A heard of giant buffalo had been stampeded toward the Berserkers. The giant buffalo trampled over the large wolfhounds that turned to flee in the opposite direction. Leif and Iggle stood in disbelief as the stampeding giant buffalo herd came charging straight at them.

"Run," Leif shouted to his men.

The Berserkers stood in disbelief of the sight they looked upon. The giant buffalo began to vent their anger on the Vikings and the wolfhounds. The enormous beast impaled and trampled the hypnotized soldiers and dogs.

"Battle-axes," shouted Leif as he stepped out and took the head off of one of the buffalo.

Iggle and Erik Blood Ax moved out to meet the giant buffalo as well. Soon Forten the Skull Splitter began to wield his ax. The Berserkers began to cut through the giant buffalo like butchers carving steaks. After a while the giant buffalo heard lay butchered on the frozen lake.

The Vikings had killed all of the giant buffalo of this small herd. Most of the wolfhounds had been killed by the giant buffalo as had a good number of Berserkers.

Leif and Iggle looked up for an enemy that was nowhere to be seen. The Berserkers were thirsty for the kill. They began to howl and lament over the loss of the wolfhounds. They showed less grief for their fallen comrades. They would be going to Valhalla. It was dog who mankind's best friend. When a Viking was in need of a friend he would get a dog. The tears flowed in torrents for the loss of the dogs.

"My dog, my dog," cried one of the Berserkers like a baby. "Buzau, poor Buzau. I am going to get them for you. I swear by Odin. Buzau you shall be avenged."

The warriors had vanished out of sight and left no trace. They had taken up a position a few kilometers away waiting for the next opportunity to assault. The Berserkers butchered the buffalo and they adorned themselves with horns and skins as new apparel. Now they were attired as wolves, bears, and giant buffalo.

The Berserkers continued their march toward the mine fields of Aztalan. This time they carried their swords and battle-axes at the ready. They held the remaining wolfhounds on leashes close to them.

The army appeared on a clearing on the edge of the lake. The challenge was made. Heluska was standing his ground as a powerful mountain this time. The warriors would test the skills of the Berserkers in the open, and in hand to hand combat.

Forten the Skull Splitter stepped into the front with battle-ax at the ready to meet Heluska. The giant red breaded Viking made his charge running head long in attack. Heluska stood waiting with blade and tomahawk at the ready. The big Viking unleashed his skull splitting ax which was tied to a rope into the air. Forten swung his mighty blade at Heluska.

The razor sharp blade ripped the air splitting the molecules. Heluska followed the path of the ax with his eyes transfixed. He bent over backward as the flying ax cut the air within a centimeter of his nose. He stood back up untouched. He then launched his own attack on the fierce Berserker.

Forten drew his sword to engage Heluska. Forten's strategy was a direct frontal assault. Heluska moved in stillness as the Viking drew within reach. Heluska began to trap, receive, and counterattack his way through the large powerful blows of Forten. He moved

Whispers of a Man

before the Viking tried to move. His pyramid nine techniques flowed like the continuous reeling of silk. He moved with the power of a great river. He rolled on unceasingly. He describe a deadly pyramid with his blades.

Forten only felt the slightest of sensation as Heluska bisected the tendon behind his left knee. Then Heluska began to employ the pyramid nine techniques. He cut off one of Forten's fingers then another. Forten was forced to drop the sword that he could not hold. He picked up his weapon with his left hand and struggled to support himself on his right leg. Forten was incensed by the deceptive tactics of Heluska.

"I am going to wear your skin for a coat you snake," said Forten to Heluska.

Heluska smiled as he serpentined his way through the defenses of Forten. Forten attacked while Heluska punctured his right eyeball with a thrust of his knife while he pretended to retreat. The large Viking screamed in agonizing pain. Heluska then described the pyramid as he cut his way into Forten's body. He stabbed Forten nine times and slashed him with cuts to connect the punctures. He then cut the tendon behind Forten right knee.

"My name is Heluska." The giant red bearded Berserker dropped to his knees. Heluska brought his tomahawk down into and through the top of his Forten's skull and cut his throat with his blade. Forten died on his knees.

Heluska stood over the fallen Berserker and gave a victory shout toward the other Vikings. The Vikings stood in silence and awe as they witness Heluska destroy one of their most powerful soldiers. The war party emerged as if from out of nowhere to engage the Berserkers. The Berserkers let loose a violent and bloodthirsty howl and came running with axes and swords raised.

Their eyes were as red as burning embers. The Earth shook beneath their feet as they approached. The bloodcurdling screams of the Berserkers and the howling of the remaining wolfhounds sent more chill through the air. It became colder.

The warriors and the Berserkers engaged. Leif, Iggle, and the rest began to cut and rip a path through the warrior ranks. Heads, arms, and bodies began flying about as if in a whirlwind. The warriors fought bravely employing the pyramid nine techniques.

Enapay, Cheveyo, and Kitchi circled and maneuvered their way into and around the bodies of the Berserkers. Heluska stood directly in the middle of the field dominating it. He cut angles through the defenses of the Vikings. He found angles in their direct frontal assault.

All around men began to drop. Everyone cut or was being cut. The warriors were in the field without regard to their own lives. The distance between any two fighters became insignificant. All had surrendered fate to destiny.

The Berserkers wielded swords and battle-axes with impunity. The battle continued to be waged. The warriors of "the people" fought bravely. The Berserkers proved to be the more seasoned of fighters. Their strength and experience began to manifest itself. With a surge the Berserkers began to overpower the warriors. In heat of the battle on the bloodstained the frozen lake the warriors began to fall.

"Kitchi," yelled Cheveyo to his brother who was in battle with a Viking. A second soldier prepared to bring his mighty ax down. Cheveyo sent his knife flying into the throat of the soldier. Kitchi cut the bowel of his opponent.

"Let's go," shouted Heluska.

The war party began its retreat. They had been beaten and practically destroyed in a single battle. As they ran the Berserkers let lose the wolfhounds. The vicious dogs took down fleeing warriors ripping out their throats.

A wolfhound took its aim on Enapay. The warrior turned to face the menacing animal. With knife in hand he met the charge and pounce of the wild dog in the same way that he had met the charge and pounce of the giant buffalo. He lowered his level and impaled the animal.

The Berserkers continued to pursue the retreating warriors. They warriors led the Viking through a field of traps. Another Berserker was impaled by spikes. The Berserkers stopped their pursuit. The warriors escaped.

The army continued to retreat back toward the Mississippi. The initial battle for the mine fields was a lost. The Vikings had taken possession of a large reserve of iron ore, copper, and uranium. The Great Mongol had secured the northern part of Aztalan and Anahuac.

The Berserkers took great pleasure in torture and mutilation. The wounded were shown no mercy. The merciless appeared in the field gouging out the eyes of the wounded and throwing them to the dogs. The Viking laughed at the moans of the wounded. They went through and hacked to death all who remained alive.

The survivors made their way back to the head of the river. There they met the war party headed by Tidasi. They had lost more than half of their numbers. Of these who did survive many were wounded severely. Only perhaps one third of the original number were still fit for battle. This day "the people" had learned a hard lesson. They had seen the wages of war. They had felt the abrupt end of a thrashing. They had lost and it there was no denying it.

"Cheveyo, Kitchi," Tidasi said relieved to see his younger brothers. "Enapay."

"We have lost the battle," stated Heluska.

"This will be a long war," Tidasi said to his friend. "It is far from over."

"You are right. The battle was difficult and bloody. We lost many today," said Heluska.

"So did they," Enapay added.

"The Earth will attest to our bravery today," said Heluska.

"They have taken the some of the fields but keeping them will prove more difficult," said Tidasi. "The fields are too large for them to control indefinitely."

"They are so many of them," Heluska reported.

"We must control the river. The Mongols are approaching from the west and more Vikings come from the east. Reinforcements are arriving every day. Cahokia has increased in population five fold. We must stop them here. We are moving one hundred thousand warriors to protect the river."

"The people" began to fortify the city with a wall. They cut down all of the trees in the vicinity of Cahokia so they could clearly see the field. The city began to take the shape of an armed camp complete with twenty-meter wall and moat.

The key to Anahuac from the north lay in controlling the river. If the river were lost the war would be lost. The battle for the Mississippi was no less important than the defense of Cahokia. The lost of the mine fields of the north was not insignificant. However, Aztalan was a rich land with vast reserves. There were mines in operation throughout the land. The lost of the fields would serve to balance the ability to produce weapons locally.

Tidasi and Heluska worked feverishly making calculations for the defense of the river system. They analyzed the tactics that the Viking had employed. The "the people" began to realize that the strengths lay in the past. They began to conduct experiments that included "red mercury" as a catalyst.

"The people" began to envision themselves from a different perspective. The Great Horde would have to begin to contend with the more technologically advance civilization. The engineers and scientists were engaged in full research and development of weapons of war. They devised diverse ways to destroy mankind. The scientists began to explore the enrichment and excitation of the minerals and resources at hand.

The scientists of Cahokia began to experiment with cinnabar and uranium. The calculations suggested that cinnabar, also known as "red mercury", acted as a catalyst in the production of enriched molecularly unstable uranium. They were able to cause control explosions at the atomic level.

Chapter 11

The Mongols had fought their way into Missouri. "The people" of Missouri stood before the Batachikan in defiance. The Missouri were a strong, proud people. The warriors possessed physical power that was equal to those of Cahokia. Tens of thousands of warriors went forth to meet the challenge of the Great Mongol.

Naran and Saran marched at the head of the army and Batachikan commanded the Great Horde which had just defeated the warriors of the Omaha. Omaha were a powerful nation whose land the Mongols had entered following the Makkah. The battle for the northwest of Anahuac had been waged during the bitter cold of the winter.

The Mongols had forced a change in nature with the invasion. They had shown that their reputation was well deserved. The Sun and the Moon, known as Naran and Saran, began to become legend in Anahuac. The tactics that they employed were held in awe by the warriors who encountered them.

A group of refugees from among "the people" of the Mississippi Valley gathered the most athletic and powerful of the men and women and formed themselves into an elite fighting force called the Chickasaw. This elite group of fighters were an amalgamation of many of the strongest warriors from east and west side of the Mississippi.

The Chickasaw stood in line with the Iowa, Osage, and Missouri to oppose the Mongols. "The people" stood on the field of battle waiting for the Horde. The Mongols had been receiving a continuous reinforcements of soldiers since they had taken occupation the northwest.

The battle began when Batachikan sent ten thousand on horseback as a shock. The Chickasaw and Missouri met them. The viciousness of the battle was evidence by the river flowing with blood. Naran and Saran engaged the Chickasaw. The two stood centered in the midst of the battle seeking all who could come within distance. Swords cut limbs from bodies and arrows pierced the hearts.

Death stood over the whole field of battle witnessing the mayhem taking place. Batachikan stood in the field killing all that he could. His guard stood before giving their lives for his protection. The battle waged on.

The were Missouri locked in battle with the Mongol assault on its flank. The Mongols arrows found many targets that day. The large men of the Missouri entered the midst of the enemy. They wielded the newly developed weapons and techniques. The Mongols began to feel themselves physically repulsed by the offensive of the Missouri. Batachikan order Saran to reinforce the soldiers fighting the Missouri. Saran dismounted his horse to get within distance of a blade.

The Missouri amir, Masou, fought against the Mongol soldiers as if he were going to live forever. His warriors stood by him in defiance of Saran. Saran moved to engage the warrior. The two wasted no time in drawing close to other. Saran and Masou clashed in violent inclusion. The pyramid nine techniques were confusing to Saran. This was his first encounter with someone who was expertly trained in this way.

The blade and tomahawk were vented at Saran. The Mongol wielded his own double blade attack against Masou. The two attacked and countered with unsurpassed prejudice. The amir's physical size was greater than Saran, however, his physical strength was not. Saran played with the large warrior as if he were playing with a toy. After a time of the playing with his large adversary he simply took his head off with blow that the Masou did not see coming.

The Mongols that began to overpower the Missouri who fought with all that they had. The Mongols had successfully split the line of the Missouri. The Chickasaw continued to fight against the invaders. They had been able to hold their own in the fight. Again the Chickasaw surged into the ranks of the Mongols. Naran and Batachikan pushed back the offensive. Saran soon rejoined the fight after he had routed the Missouri.

Naran and Saran united their forces and began to surround the Chickasaw. Then the warriors of the Chickasaw began to abandon all hope of survival and counterattacked once more. Soldiers and warriors fell on all sides. There lay tens of thousands in the field of battle. The Chickasaw were relentless in the pursuit of battle. And the Mongols kept coming.

Soon the Mongols began to take more casualties. The Chickasaw were not to be stopped in their vented violence. They enjoyed the fight as much as the Mongols. Batachikan continued to order his men to crush the Chickasaw. He saw more and more of his men killed. He then gave the order to send all of his men against the Chickasaw in a concerted effort to wipe them out completely. Again the Chickasaw repulsed the attack. The fight waged long into the night and into the next day.

Many Chickasaw fell during the battle but their fervor did not diminish. When one of the Chickasaw went down two more took his place. Batachikan saw the a better recourse was to go around the Chickasaw lands and to avoid further conflict with these Spartan like warriors.

Batachikan upon seeing that a direct assault against the Chickasaw was more costly than he had calculated. He decided to change his tactical route. The Chickasaw did not pursue the Mongols but headed back to face the Vikings and Celts who were approaching from the rear. The Chickasaw had determined to make their region an area where none could or would dare to enter. They would gather to meet the Vikings and Celts in Kentucky. The Chickasaw continued to wage war violently. Their reputation began to spread. Soon all of nations had shock warriors trained in the Chickasaw way. They trained in the way of absence of fear of death in the face of the enemy.

Batachikan had expected casualties but he had not expected to encounter the Chickasaw. The Missouri had been a powerful force in their own right. They had been in the mold of the other nations which had been conquered. The Chickasaw seemed to enjoy the battle as much as Naran and Saran. Batachikan foresaw that this nation would never bow.

The closer the Mongols got to Cahokia the greater the resistance that they found. They found protecting the Mississippi more than two hundred thousand men. Batachikan sent forces led by Naran and Saran to meet the challenge. "The people" considered this to be death ground. And like the Chickasaw they fought to the death. A rolling wave of blades rippled its way toward the Mongol Horde.

Into the ferocity of the fire did "the people" and the Mongols enter. The battle waged on for four days. The bodies covered the fields. Horses, giant deer and buffalo lay wasted in the field as well. Everything in the line of sight was gone. Every life that had breathe the air of the days before was now lifeless.

Batachikan surveyed the land that lay wasted in his line of sight. How could this be the same land of great beauty and abundance that he had come to know not so long ago? There was no peace. Everything bore a scare. The earth beneath his feet screamed out in agony to him. He could hear the voices of the countless moaning in the agony of their mutilated remains. He had wanted to spare this land of the cost of continued war. He had wanted to taste the sweet waters and fruits that had run freely and grown wild. He knew the scares on the face of Anahuac and the land would not heal quickly. He looked up to see the glistening Great Pyramid of Cahokia.

Chapter 12

There came visitors to the gates of Cahokia. It was a small band of Mongol soldiers. "The people" immediately sounded the alarm. It was a messenger from Batachikan. He was giving "the people" a last opportunity to end the confrontation.

"The Mongols do not want further hostilities. We seek only to pass through your lands to the eastern wilderness and settle in those sparsely inhabited lands," said the messenger.

"Why do you attack our people and confiscate our lands?" asked Hiamovi.

"We only want peace. Will you let us settle in the eastern wilderness? We will be your neighbors and friends," the messenger further stated.

"'The people' will take this under consideration," Hiamovi said to the Batachikan's messenger.

"If we give them land in the eastern wilderness perhaps we can gain an end to this war," said Matawau.

"We will have to open our doors wide open for them to walk right in," said Hiamovi.

"Once they are in will they ever leave," said Nosh. "If we are stupid we will do this."

"We have a chance to end this war now," said the Matawau.

The council of Cahokia convened to deliberate and vote on the issue of allowing the Mongols to pass through their lands. The council now allowed delegates from the Mengwe to speak and have a voted in the decisions of the state. The action seemed to appease the refugees who had flooded into the city. They now had representation from among the Mengwe whom they saw like themselves as refugees.

"We cannot allow them to enter our lands," warned Tidasi who had returned from the north. "This would a very bad tactical error."

"If we allow them into our precincts this would be the same as poisoning our own wells," said Nosh.

The vote was taken and counted. The Mongols would be allowed passages through the precincts of Cahokia to the eastern wilderness. Batachikan was given word of the decision. He began to think that Hiamovi had reconsidered.

"We cannot allow this to happen," said Tidasi.

"The vote has been cast," said Matawau.

Tidasi pounded his fists on the council table and said, "You have misled 'the people'. Your cowardice will make slaves of us all."

"'The people' are deluded by fear," stated Hiamovi.

"We must finish them. There will be no second chances," said Nosh.

"We will let them enter Cahokia but they will not leave," said Tidasi.

The Mongols were told that they must enter the land of Cahokia unarmed and on foot. They were also told that they should not tarry longer than twenty-four hours at any single location. Batachikan would be among the last to cross the river. He stood in the distance observing as his soldiers began their crossing. Soon more than half of his army had crossed the river and were stationed on the opposite bank.

Then there was a sudden movement. The warriors of "the people" began to attack the Mongols. The warriors had begun to attack the Mongols while one half of the army was still in the water. The Mongols on the shore were on foot without weapons. The warriors of "the people" began to slaughter them in their places.

Each Mongol on the east shore of the river died under the blade that day. Batachikan, betrayed, watched in disbelief as his men were slaughtered. There was nothing that could be done. They had entered Cahokia with no weapons and the river was to their backs. The carnage inflicted on the Mongols was unimaginable. The warriors of "the people" began to show a likeness to their adversaries in their ruthlessness.

Naran and Saran stood watching as their soldiers were killed in their eyesight. The soldiers who were still in the water were ordered to the fallback to the opposite shore. This was a stunning defeat for the Mongols. And "the people" took no prisoners that day. Each Mongol soldier was killed and mutilated before the eyes of Batachikan, Naran, and Saran. The three stood silent as the soldiers were slaughtered.

Batachikan gave the order for men to fall back. The Great Horde had suffered a devastating defeat that day. This was a betrayal that Batachikan could not image that Hiamovi and "the people" were capable. Naran and Saran said nothing. This was more than a provocation. Now it would be all-out war and with no hope for peace. They knew that "the people" would now have to engage in the dance of the warrior. From this dance there would be no repose. From this pain there would be no abatement. This was now in its purest essence a war. And it would end when one side was destroyed. To Naran and Saran this was as it should be.

Chapter 13

The Vikings, the Welsh, and the Celts all pushed from the east. They continued to find little opposition as the marched through the lands. The land opened up to them and allow entrance. Then they entered the field at Kentucky. They saw a land filled with the richness of abundance. There were giant deer and buffalo everywhere. The waters of the land offered sweetness and flavor.

The land appeared to be uninhabited. "The people" had all evacuated ahead of the invading soldiers of the Horde. The Vikings, Welsh, and Celts took up camp in Kentucky. The unoccupied land would be a provide a buttress in the south. The Golden Horde would take this land forever as a tribute to the Great Khan. This would surely be worthy of reward and an allotment in Anahuac.

"They are here," said Shoteka, the amir of the Chickasaw. "We will not run or retreat. This is where they lose." This Chickasaw amir did not like the idea of trespassers let alone invaders. Many of the Chickasaw had been forced east by the Mongol assault in the west. They had retreated to the river and had come to occupy both sides. Now the Vikings were approaching from the east. The Chickasaw would defend, hold, and fight to the death.

Fighting to the death is what gave men supernatural power. Fighting to the death made men capable of fantastic feats. Fighting to the death was the absence of fear in the face of one's own death. Fighting to the death was a virtue on the path to immortality. They looked into the face of death and relished in it.

Shoteka smelled the air and commented, "They smell awful and filthy. They smell like wet dogs."

The Chickasaw considered the Vikings and their company to be a foul species who were interloping in the land. They were driven by a completely radical solution to the problem. They would kill everyone. This seemed to make sense because they realized that it was simply to many invaders to negotiate with and they were wrong. So the Chickasaw would take no prisoners ever. They developed the sense of smell for the Viking locations. Instinctively they found themselves facing the enemy by just thinking of it. They loved to fight and crush the enemy.

"I love to fight the enemy," said a warrior.

"I love to crush him," said another. They were an army composed of the dispossessed who drew into a great cluster to fight and die together for the sake and honor of "the people".

"Quickly lets move," said the Viking thirsty Shoteka. A wave began to ripple through the forest. The birds began to stir and the wind began to whip. There came a rain of arrows and lances upon the Horde. Then the golden-brown bombers went to work. The Chickasaw had a special affinity for the knob head war club in addition to the blade and tomahawk. They Chickasaw warriors poured into the valley where the Vikings, Welsh, and Celts lie in wait. They suddenly appeared out of the wall of the forest face. The Horde gave a fierce shout of defiance.

The battle was on. Chickasaw warriors poured into the land like running water. They swarmed from everywhere. The Viking became confused with their pattern of attack. No Viking found himself fighting a single warrior, or maybe the one seemed to be many.

The Chickasaw fighting prowess lay in the application of the pyramid. Each warrior in a five man bimiba would cut across the field to a specified point outlining a pyramid. Then he would continue based on the changes that happened as a result. The bimiba held their continuity within the war party but was allowed to infinitely create within its pyramid. The Vikings had no defense for this offense.

The Chickasaw attacked with an intensity that the Vikings thought that only they could wield. The two groups battled in the midst of death. Warriors and soldiers fell by the hundreds on both sides. The bodies lay everywhere and the ground became blood soaked.

There was so much blood spilled that day that the ground could hold no more. Everywhere there were pools of blood.

"So you are a monster to be feared. See me, fear me I am Chickasaw," a Chickasaw warrior said before crushing a Celtic head.

The Chickasaw did not relent nor did they stop coming. All over Kentucky burial mounds began to transform the land. Soon there were hundreds of them dotting the landscape. The Chickasaw still attacked any and all that they encountered. The Viking, Welsh, and Celts grew to fear the relentless Chickasaw.

The Vikings began to create new ways to torture their captives. "You Chickasaw are very brave. And nothing can make you scream. Try this," said one of the soldiers as he castrated a warrior. The warrior did not scream.

The Vikings saw the Chickasaw as the most ruthless and relentless of the warriors that they had ever encountered anywhere. The word spread of the battle that had taken place in Kentucky. All now knew that none could enter the land and not have their feet covered with blood. Soon Kentucky was abandoned because the land was saturated with blood. Superstitions began to grow and the ghost became specters moving in the night. And the animals did not come.

What was left of the mixed contingent of Vikings, Welsh, and Celts continued to move northward toward Cahokia. The Chickasaw continued to kill them along the way. The Vikings rarely, if ever, saw their enemies. They only saw the fellows fall. This was the way of the Chickasaw.

They Chickasaw took control and added to their territories. They also took possession of Kentucky as a trophy. Although this land would be uninhabitable for many years to come they lay claim to it and posted warning signs to acclaim what would become of trespassers from the Northern Horde. The Northern Horde was given no retreat and no regress.

Batachikan stood silent as he surveyed his army. He would now give the order to attack Cahokia from the west, north and east. The battle for Cahokia was to begun. The Berserkers in the north had been grinding their battle-axes waiting for the opportunity to join the main onslaught. Out of the dark waste land of the north they had come to take possession of the mine fields of Aztalan.

Tidasi led his army of ten thousand past the head of the great river to do battle. This time they were armed with new weapons. His warriors had been supplied with the new red mercury triggered high explosives. The bimiba led by Enapay was given the task of slipping behind the enemy lines and destroying the ability of the Northern Horde to manufacture weapons locally. The iron mines must be shut down.

The main war party waited at the head of the great river. The Berserkers waited for the opportunity to avenge the dogs and Forten. Tidasi stood in plain view. Once again the Berserkers unleashed the dogs in an assault. Again there was thunder heard rumbling toward the Vikings.

"There will be meat for all tonight," shouted Leif.

The Berserkers then suspended their axes from ropes as they began slicing giant buffaloes with the centrifugal force. The buffalo were wiped out almost immediately. The dogs of the Berserkers fared no better. The war party cut the throats of all the animals. All the animal warriors and soldiers from both sides fell.

Then the two groups faced one another ready to do battle. The Berserkers let loose their most bloodcurdling howl and the warriors shouted in reply. The two joined together in combat. The warriors entered within the reach of the Berserkers wielding tomahawks, blades, and the pyramid nine techniques. The Vikings entered the field with their heavy, powerful, and deadly weapons.

"Attack," Tidasi shouted to the army.

"He is mine," said Iggle pointing at Tidasi.

The battle was engaged. This time the warriors of "the people" were more prepared than before. They believed in the new weapons that had been developed. They all had come to believe in the battle tactics and especially the pyramid nine techniques they employed.

Soon the battle was joined and the living became the dead. Tidasi maneuvered his way in and out of the path of falling axes. He avoided the iron hammers and cut the leg tendons of many. Iggle continued to search out Tidasi in the field. He but simply had to following the whirlwind of slinging blades that sliced through everything before them.

Iggle stood before Tidasi. Tidasi locked his gaze as a hawk focusing on a single bird. And like a swooping bird of prey he dove for his victim. His movement was that of a blinding flash of light. Iggle had extinguished many lights in his days. His giant ax cut through the air close to Tidasi but never cut close enough. Iggle moved always to where Tidasi was but never where he was going to be.

Again Iggle swung his mighty ax with the intention to take the head of Tidasi. Then Iggle felt a small sensation. He looked at his hand to see that a finger was missing. He grew more mad and incensed. He drew closer to Tidasi with his weapon raised. This time his assault was more focused on the intention of killing.

Tidasi also held Iggle in disdain. He saw Iggle as a crude attempt at humanity by barbarians. He could never imagine that such as Iggle could approach him on any level. There would be no parlay between them.

Iggle moved circumspectly stalking Tidasi. The intensity of attack was all consuming. He was the epitome of a bad dream. He became a monster coming on a cold winter's day. His ax came closer at each swing.

Tidasi knew that retreat was not an option for him. He stepped into the onslaught of Iggle. He moved inside the eye of the storm. In close and inside of Iggle's powerful stroke Tidasi found calm. He stood close enough to embrace Iggle. He wrapped the big Viking in a body lock and launched him into the air. Iggle slammed into the icy ground very hard. Tidasi's throw dislodged his shoulder from the joint.

He followed Iggle in his flight through the air. He held his blade and tomahawk at the ready for a malevolent landing. He soared like an eagle with its talons extended. Iggle turned to see Tidasi in flight but could not raise his ax. Leif launched himself at Tidasi. His large body impacted Tidasi in mid flight like a missile and diverted him from his course.

Iggle struggled back up to his feet holding his ax in the other hand. This time Tidasi was confronted by two berserk Vikings. Again he step into their midst. He could sense that his army though fighting valiantly were still no match for the Berserkers. In his mind's eye he could see the entire field. He saw his brother warriors being slain.

A wave of vibrancy entered the field of battle. There was a new force coming into play. It was Heluska's war party joining the fight. Tidasi's war party was rejuvenated by the new energy that was interjected. Heluska step into the midst of Tidasi's battle with Iggle and Leif. Now the one-armed Iggle found himself in lone battle with Heluska.

"Heluska, happy to see you brother," said Tidasi.

"Would not have missed it for the world," Heluska said while cutting through a soldier.

Leif squared off to face Tidasi. Tidasi entered into the assault of Leif thrusting his foot him into the Viking's abdomen sending back and down on the ice. Ivar Bones and Olaf the Stout joined the battle to help Iggle and Leif. Now they were four against two. Tidasi and Heluska entered fight with the four.

Olaf stepped in to aid Iggle against Heluska. The three became locked in battle. Heluska assumed the posture of jaguar battling two bears. His blades ripped and cut. He stepped inside Olaf's stoke utilizing the pyramid nine techniques inflicting the tiny cuts all over his body. Iggle vainly attempted to chop off the head of Heluska. Heluska cut off another of Iggle's fingers.

"Two of my fingers. You bastard." Heluska continued to step in the storm of Olaf inflicting tiny razor cuts until Olaf was covered in blood. Blood ran down his face and into his eyes. He swung his ax and hit nothing but air.

Leif and Ivar pursued Tidasi attempting to catch him as they could. Tidasi stood before the two like a mountain and when he moved he moved like a great river. He moved so there was never a line for the two to attack simultaneously. He managed to keep one them in front of the other and off balance. They fought in vain and to their own frustration.

Tidasi slashed his way into doorway of Ivar's defense and punctured his abdomen. He brought his tomahawk down through Leif's foot as he made another swing of the ax miss. Like a tornado he turn his stab into a slice and continued disemboweling Ivar. The Viking stood in shock watching his intestines fall to the ground. Ivar scream in agony as tried to collect his innards from the bloody ice pack and put them back in.

Leif continued to wage against Tidasi. Tidasi always moved just a split second before Leif tried to move while he made another cut to Leif body. Leif pursued Tidasi but found himself unable to catch him. And when he attempted to evade he always found Tidasi next to him. Tidasi's blade cut clean and cold through Leif's forehead. Blood poured into eyes blocking his vision.

Tidasi moved in close to Ivar. Ivar barely felt it as Tidasi wound himself around him to cut his throat. Ivar was dead before he hit the ground. Seeing everything he zeroed in on Leif. More Berserkers joined to help the struggling Leif. Tidasi continued to see everything, including those who joined the fight.

He moved threw the Vikings puncturing the throats of all who brought themselves within reach of his blade. Tidasi ensured that they met their ends swiftly. He continued to cut them in the place that killed them instantly, their throats. Tidasi became transformed in his assault on the Northerners. He began to see everything in slow motion. He had somehow transcended time and could see three, four, or five movements ahead. He became a killing machine. He was an emotionless killing machine.

Heluska continued to make a thousand cuts to the person of Olaf the Stout. Olaf stood bleeding from every part of his body except the bottom of his feet. He felt no pain only well ventilated. The cold air touched all the nerve endings. He began to shiver uncontrollably and started to shake. He dropped his ax. The blood had pour from his body into the snow covering ground. He stood in a pool of his own blood. Clutching his own person he continued to shiver and shake uncontrollably until he dropped dead.

The warriors began to hold their own against the Berserkers. Though they were still not the caliber of soldier that the Vikings were their spirit, tenacity, and bravery held them up. The warriors found themselves far more agile than their adversaries. They could readily outmaneuver the clumsy Northerners.

They believed in the techniques in which they had been trained. They began to have faith in the art that they practiced. Once they had developed faith in the pyramid nine techniques they began to overcome fear of death. Once they had overcome the fear of death they could stand face to face with death. They stood before death a fierce fighting force that did not wince. Now they were the warriors of "the people".

The Berserkers though battle hardened and combat ready could not overwhelm the warriors with their patented surge. Again and again they attempted to break the backs and spirits of the warriors. Again and again the warriors repulsed the attack. The Berserkers numbers were now more than doubled the warriors.

Leif gave the command for a full surge into the field of battle. He realized that this was the best of what the "the people" had to offer in resistance. Now was a time to crush the enemy once and for all. The Berserkers came in an endless wave. They fell like giant hail stones upon the warriors. Iron hammers and axes began to break through the defenses of the defenders of Aztalan.

Tidasi could see that if his men did not retreat now then his entire army might be crushed here. He gave the command to retreat. The warriors began the their descent toward the head of the river. The retreat was orderly. The warriors set up skirmish lines so those who were falling back would not be caught from behind. The Berserkers did not relent. Fresh soldiers continued to attack. The wounded soldiers retired back to the encampment. Any wounded warrior who lie was executed without hesitation.

The Berserkers continued the surge into the mine fields. There was absolutely no resistance to the occupation. The miners were not warriors and had not been trained for battle. Most of them had already gone south to join "the people's" army.

An objective of the Great Mongol had been realized. They had taken the mine fields and the mining technologies. The spoils of war included the cities and towns of the region. The Vikings were in complete control of the northern territories of Aztalan.

Iggle and Leif struggled from the field as well. Both of them were bloody and severely injured. The other Berserkers fared little better. There had been many injuries and deaths. They moved into mines to take complete possession for the Great Mongol. The Wisconsin, Minnesota, and Michigan lands contained many cities and towns. In the northern climate the Vikings founds themselves in a comfort zone. Now the process for creating a Mongol state was to begin.

Chapter 14

Though the fighting spirit of warriors of "the people" had not suffered their numbers did. Half of their numbers had been killed or injured and they had lost the mines of the north. These mines were a vast concentration of resources. Now most of world's vast resource of copper was under the control of the Mongols. Not to mention the iron ore, cinnabar, and uranium deposits.

The dead warriors were buried in mounds and the injured were sent back to Cahokia. Both sides of this conflict were now aware that this would be no short war. Many more volunteers continued to arrive. The Great Mongol had greatly over estimated their capacity to take Aztalan rapidly. They had imagined that "the people" would fall to their knees once they saw the power of the Great Horde.

The Great Khan was intolerant of failure on the part of his generals. He sent messengers to Batachikan demanding a full progress report. And the Great Khan ordered more reinforcements from the Russian and Nordic regions of Asia. New conscripts were called from all regions of the Mongol Empire. The blood tax was raised on every family within the empire. The Viking numbers were replenished rapidly.

The warriors of "the people" also continued to receive volunteers from all over Kemanahuac. For every one that fell two more would come forth to replace him. The Northern Horde had grossly underestimated the character of the warrior spirit among "the people"

Tidasi and Heluska rapidly integrated the newly arriving volunteer into war parties and further dividing the war parties into group of bimibas. There was no time for long formal training. A two-week training program was devised, and then it was off to battle. Veterans of battle began to take on the roles of trainers in the art of war. After a short period each new warrior was assigned to a bimiba and sent in to the field. It was in the field that each volunteer would be trained under fire.

"They are children," said Heluska.

"They are young men. This war is really all about them. We are fighting for them not them for us," Tidasi replied.

In this war it was the old who were the primary warriors. These were the ones who had lived, seen, and experienced enough of life to take it in to battle. To be a warrior was a great honor. There was no conscription and all came forward of their own accord. They young wanted to earn their place in the ranks of men.

The women of Cahokia were also formed into combat, and reconnaissance bimibas. They became particularly acute in the art of stealth. They would spend weeks in the forest hiding and waiting. Then would suddenly appear and then disappear after cutting the throats of a clueless enemy.

"Look what we've got here," a solider said while bringing in a woman warrior posing as a weak and helpless girl. "I will put you on a leash. You are with me now, whore."

The soldier led her away to have his way with her. He took her in to the darkness of his tent. As he lay down his sword and ax she cut his throat, and disappeared silently in to the night. This is the way of the female warrior.

Tidasi studied the faces of the volunteers. There were no age restrictions. Some of the warriors were old men while some were boys. Some bimibas included grandfather, father, and son. He saw exuberance in their faces. He knew that many youths would never return home from battle. He also knew that many of the old men would never return to be the heads of their families again either.

"You are all very brave. To be brave is not the mere act of having come here, but to be brave is to know that at any moment we may fall and still we come. Those of you who are old will return home to provide leadership for our people and fight at the last stand if needed. Those who are young will return home to provide security for our people and wait until we call for you. The rest will fight now,"

Tidasi said dividing the men according to their abilities.

To avoid losses of entire families Tidasi ordered that no bimiba could have more than three members from the same family. This still did not guarantee that any family would continue. It was only hope that some members of a family would survive. He knew that the deaths of all the males members of a family would be devastating. And how could he forget his own three younger brothers who were somewhere in the northern territories. Knowing what the loss of his own brothers would mean to his family made him remember to consider all families. His heart raced each time he heard of casualties or saw an injured warrior being carried in.

*****

Enapay, Cheveyo, Kitchi, and the other members of the bimiba hid themselves well in the forest of the behind enemy lines. They blended into the scenery and took on the smell of the environment. They knew well the migration patterns of the animals and they moved within those patterns. They moved by night and watched by day. They studied the patterns of the Vikings. They saw that the Vikings consumed much uncooked meat and drank alcohol constantly. It was the vile combination of blood and spirits that gave an edge to their ugliness.

In the night they saw the pale faced barbarians as specters anguishing in their drunkenness. Enapay stole up close enough to a sleeping Berserker to smell the stench of bad breath. His loathing for the colorless form and foul odor was enough for him to know that he could never dream of sharing even the air with them. He had heard the stories of the Northerners having been born of the caves of Caucasia. He had heard that the were raised by and lived with dogs. He could smell the dog in each of them. He was revolted by the site of them.

He sat watching the drunken Viking sleep. He restrained himself to keep from cutting throat of the wasted barbarian. Enapay felt that he could slit a thousand drunkened throats in a single night. That was not his mission. He jobs was to destroy access to the mines and eliminate the logistics of weapons manufacture.

He also saw in their drunkenness that men lay with each other. This was an unimaginable practice that was unheard of in Aztalan. He sat listening as the men lay together in their ghastly imaginations. Enapay saw this vile rejection of humanity in their wildest machinations. The more he observed of their behaviors the more they revolted him.

He moved his bimiba further behind enemy lines. The land was empty of "the people" and only barbarians persisted. The heart of the mining area was a narrow neck of land that separated the northern sea from the Michigan Valley. It was in the Michigan Valley where the majority of the cities of the north were located. If a chasm was created in the narrow neck of land then the entire valley would be flooded and majority of the Viking Army would be drowned, and so would the mines. Enapay would send a watery destruction upon the Golden Horde.

The bimiba lost itself and became oblivious to the enemy. The Viking had no clue that their lines had been infiltrated. They only counted the spoils of war. They set about immediately to transport all the stockpiles of resources out of Aztalan. At this time there were more than a million metric tons of copper under the control of the Great Mongol. They immediately moved all the copper out of the land.

It was not copper that "the people" were interested in. It was uranium. The scientists of Cahokia been able to apply the superconductive properties of red mercury by combining it with uranium. It was the mission of Enapay's bimiba to begin the cascading chain reaction by introducing red mercury in to the largest vein of uranium in Aztalan. The ballotechnic properties of red mercury would initiate the cascade.

The Great Mongol had not yet realized the kinetic potential of uranium. Their level of science did not reach to the thermonuclear rationale. They knew nothing of the desperation that drove men to destroy everything to keep it from falling into the hands of deviants.

Enapay knew exactly where the richest resource of uranium lay. It was adjacent to a major copper mine. This copper mine was so rich that nuggets weighing up to five hundred kilograms lay as boulders. Natural wire meshes were in abundance as well, and would act as conductors for carrying an exploding wire charge through the superconductive red mercury and to the uranium. It would be exploding wire that would be the trigger. Once the materials were prepared then it would only take a pulse to trigger the exploding wire.

The bimiba stood undisturbed surveying the vast beauty of the Michigan Valley countryside. Its glistening pyramid stood equal to its counterpart in Cahokia. This valley was one of the most productive and fertile regions within Anahuac. This area had been home to hundreds of thousands of people. They were now refugees in and around Cahokia. All the urban centers of the Michigan Valley were also under the control of the Great Mongol.

The bimiba knew that by creating a fissure in the narrow neck of land that separated the northern sea from the valley would created another sea comparable to the northern sea. In addition to causing an inundation the land would become desolate, and regrettably one of the world's great industrial centers might be lost forever.

The bimiba slipped in to the darkness of the night. They had cut themselves off from the knowledge of the circumstance that were taking place. They were oblivious to everything except their mission. The bimiba focused on one point with a single minded determination to succeed. They could not separate themselves from any aspect of the world that the occupied. The were of the land. This land was their homeland.

In to the midst of the Michigan Valley they slipped undetected. They were lost in naturalness. Witnessing the holocaust that had taken place in the land they recorded all that they saw. The Viking had scorched the earth in the horrendous assault on the land and "the people". The signs of the carnage lay everywhere.

The Viking had taken prisoners. These prisoners had been enslaved and the women and children raped and abused. Executions were literally taking place continually. The Vikings brought new and more cruel ways to torture.

The members of the bimiba watched in horror the atrocities perpetrated by the Viking against "the people". The bimiba slipped in to the largest of the uranium mines. The Berserkers had neglected to safeguard the uranium mines and preferred to concentrate on iron and copper. Enapay and his team disappeared in to the void of the uranium mine.

The intricacies of the design of the fissionable explosive device was not complex. The bimiba work quietly and competently in completing the job. They packed the largest vein of uranium with red mercury and natural nickel that was readily available. The bimiba worked swiftly in the preparing the uranium mine to explode. Once the exploding wire was detonated it would act as a primary charge for the high explosion and nuclear reaction. They completed the construction of a nuclear bomb.

The only thing left for the team was to build the trigger to detonate the bomb. The only way to generated the pulse required to produce to four-million joules of energy necessary to ignite the explosion was through a lightning strike. The spring was coming soon and so would the thunder and lightning.

They built lightning rods to collect and concentrate the lighting energy of a storm to one point. The north was known for its numerous lightning strikes in the spring. The bimiba wired the mined and turned it into a primed reactor. And with a single pulse the entire region would be turned into a giant flash of fire and light.

The lightning would provide the energy to explode the nickel, exciting the red mercury, and causing a cascading reaction in the uranium, and nuclear detonation. In theory this was all plausible although this type of technology was shunned because of the memories of the war with Maya. Working as if ghost under the noses of the Berserkers the bimiba went about construction of the largest fission bomb ever made.

The bimiba also had to turned its attention to the rescue of the prisoners. This was an unexpected mission that they must also accomplish. The bomb was set and they could not simply disappear back in to the forest and leave "the people" facing torture and death. In the distance they saw the death faces of the prisoners behind the stockade walls. "The people" had never known these hardships before. It was as if a plague had been sent upon them. The men were killed in various and monstrous ways and the women and children continued to be ravaged and raped.

The screams of both men and women were audible from a great

Whispers of a Man   143

distance. The sounds that were heard were unbearable to the ears of the bimiba. They would make the move to free the prisoners now. The bimiba realized that they had an advantage in surprise. They intended to use the element of surprise to create a distraction.

In addition to the three brothers the bimiba had two other members, Bodaway and Elsu. They along with Enapay would provide the necessary distraction. Bodaway, Firemaker, would create a distraction on the other side of the camp. Elsu, Flying Falcon, would create a scene of panic enabling Enapay to free the women and children.

Then almost simultaneously the bimiba went to work. Bodaway through a mixture of saltpeter, coal, and sulfur concocted a compound of black powder and packed it tightly in a container. He moved closer to the supply cache that was stored close to the stockade. Enapay and Elsu wasted little time in stealthily cutting the throats of the two guards who had drank to much Mead. Quietly did they pulled the unsuspecting guards in to the darkness. Soon Enapay and Elsu were wearing the wolf skins of the fallen Berserkers.

"This thing smells foul," said Elsu. "How can they stand it?"

"It's them that you smell. They smell like shit," said Enapay.

Enapay lighted the wolf skin worn by Elsu. He ran so fast it seemed that he was flying. Simultaneously, Bodaway lit fused of the black powder. There was a blinding explosion and a fire roared through the supply depot in a raging blaze that was being fueled by the alcohol in the mead.

The Berserkers were completely disoriented in their drunkenness. They sight of Elsu flying like a falcon across the field in a burning wolf skin was a sight that amazed them all. They began to chase who they thought was a burning comrade up and down. Elsu moved swiftly appearing as a burning specter that streaked to and fro mesmerizing the drunken Berserkers. The fire and explosion that Bodaway had caused was now raging out of control. Soon everything was in complete chaos and in an uproar.

Enapay remained calm as he slip in to the darkness and confusion to open the stockade gate.

"What the hell is going on," asked one of the surprised Berserkers of the disguised Enapay. The next sound that heard was blade and tomahawk cutting in to this head and throat.

The frightened captives were to afraid to move. "I am Enapay, son of Nosh. Come with me."

Cheveyo and Kitchi entered the barracks where the women and children were kept. With blades in hand the two moved on the drunken Vikings who stood guard. The two did their work efficiently and expertly. The frightened women huddle in corners afraid to move.

"We are your brothers. You will not be harmed. Come," said Cheveyo.

The brothers told the women and children to hold hands. Then like a train they made their dash in to the forest as fast as they could. There were hundreds of captives. The bimiba did not realize the magnitude of the rescue attempt. It appeared to be great deal of the population of the Michigan Valley. Now they would have to lead them to safety.

It took quite some time for the Vikings to realize what was really happening. When they did realize the plan was in full motion and was happening right before their eyes. They eventually caught up with the burning Berserker and all that they found was a scorched wolf skin. They didn't discover the deception until the supply cache fire was under control. Then they discovered the bodies of those who had their throat's slit. The Viking Berserkers stood dumbfounded believing that the prisoners had somehow staged this great escape.

There had been so much confusion that "the people" had managed a sizable head start. Before long the forest were full of angry and berserk Vikings bent on revenge and on regaining their captives. The chase was on. First order was let loose the dogs. They would hunt the captives down.

The feeling of pursuit caught up with the fleeing escapees and the bimiba. The escapees found themselves continually looking back for their pursuers. "The people" instinctively began to run faster. They did not see anything when they looked back. They were running from fear. No matter how fast and far they ran fear was right behind them in pursuit.

"This where we wait. Move through."

Enapay led the bimiba and the escapees in to a natural defile. They were forced to form a single file. That meant that the Berserkers would also be force to form a single line in pursuit. The wolfhounds were the first to arrive at the defile. They dogs made no hesitation in entering in to the narrow defile where arrows filled their bodies one by one. Finally, only one wolfhound was left. He thought better than to enter the defile and turned tail and ran in the other direction.

The Berserkers continued their hot pursuit of "the people" who were fleeing. Elsu stood at the entrance to the defile waiting for the first of the Berserkers to enter. He allowed himself to be seen and pursued. Once again Elsu flew like a falcon from the plodding steps of the Viking. Then Elsu stopped and turn to face the Berserker. The Viking stood stunned before the now embolden Elsu.

"You are not one of the prisoners," said the surprised Viking.

"I am Flying Falcon of 'the people'."

Then the surprised Viking turned around to find Enapay standing to his rear. The large Viking held his sword in one hand and his ax in the other. Although alone the berserk Viking felt no apprehension at facing two weak little boys. He charged at Enapay swinging and cutting simultaneously. The Viking's cuts ripped through the dense forest. The more that he cut the more entangled he became in the vines that wrapped themselves around his weapons. Soon the Viking found himself stalled and unable to wield his mighty weapons.

Enapay moved in close with blades in hand. The Berserker release his grip on his weapons and also choose his shorter blade. Enapay moved in holding his knife with a reverse grip. As the Viking came forward lunging with his knife Enapay hooked him with his tomahawk and brought him in close enough for a piston like thrust in to his kidney. Elsu delivered a long and deep cut in to his exposed back. The two warriors played what seemed to be a game of cat and mouse with the frustrated Viking who turned again to face one then another.

Enapay drove his tomahawk deep in to cervical vertebra of the Northerner. The berserk Viking turned again to face Enapay and Elsu moved in to finish him by cutting his throat. The Viking looked at the two before he died with a look of disdain for the way that they had fought their fight. He died in the anger of knowing that they had not giving him sufficient chance to utilized his terrible tactic.

One by one the berserk Vikings entered the defile. One by one the all met the same fate. The defile turned their large numbers in to an insignificant band of individuals seeking the same end. All that entered the defile found the same fate, death by blade.

Soon no Viking would enter the defile. They realized that their was no strategically sound way for them to overcome the tactical advantage that the bimiba held. The only way for the Vikings to turn an advantage was to find a way around and surprise the bimiba from behind.

Unknown to the Berserkers the escapees were long gone. It was the bimiba who alone held the entire Viking Army at bay forcing them to fight in a defile. In fighting in the defile the Viking numbers and power of their weapons became insignificant. It was simply a series of battles of one Viking against five warriors. The Vikings could get no advantage.

The escapees made it back down to the head of the river and to safety. The bimiba continued to frustrate the Berserkers. Viking loses were beginning to prove costly. They were losing many of the their best soldiers in this terrain.

They Berserkers decided that they could not continue their pursuit in this way. The sent half of their forces to encircle the bimiba. By the time that they arrive at the other side of the defile everything and everyone was gone. Only the bodies of Viking and dogs lie in the thickets.

The women and children from among the escapees boarded barges which took them downriver to safety. The men volunteered to stay and fight for their own homes. They were intermixed with the ranks of the army. They would be able to provide invaluable logistical and tactical support for any counteroffensive that would be staged against the Berserker encampment.

The mission now would be to hold the head of the river until the spring when the lightning storms would come and the ionization of the air would be enough to trigger the exploding wire. "The people" would stage a hit and run offensive to frustrate and harass the Vikings into making mistakes and tactical errors in judgment.

Chapter 15

"The people" built walls around all the cities of the Aztalan to protect against the Mongols and Vikings from simply walking in. Forts began to dot the landscape and the land beget the castles of dreams. The legislature of "the people" created a new branch of the government for the enforcement of homeland security. They passed more laws. With each new law there were instituted statutes which impinged on the freedom that all "the people" had previously enjoyed.

More and more "the people" found themselves roused and under suspicion. The feeling of freedom that had always been known was now becoming limited to an elite few, "the people" of Cahokia. Soon there was a class structure in place. This structure insured that the citizens of Cahokia were accommodated privileges that others were not afforded.

The Mengwe continued to become more averse to the new laws. They saw themselves as no different, and one and the same people. They also had been given a status which was less than that of "the people" of Cahokia. The population of the Mengwe in Cahokia had help to swell the city to more than five times its original population.

The Mengwe volunteers had come forth in great numbers to fight the enemy. Now they found themselves in a political battle for equality in their own homeland. They found themselves challenged in matters of freedom and oppression. They grew more frustrated and angry.

The freedom that had been known throughout in Anahuac was vanishing. The Mongols had begun a campaign of rumors and propaganda. Soon there were so many stories going around that the truth soon became disjunctive and sparse. After a while the difference between truth and falsehood became indiscernible.

"We are being controlled by fear," said Hiamovi to Nosh. "We are succumbing to their psychology."

"Yes, you are right, Ku Tu."

"Suspicion is a mighty weapon against us. They will not have to defeat us with their swords and arrows. We are defeating ourselves."

"We must stop this psychological warfare, but how?" asked Nosh.

"We are designing our own downfall. This new legislation is destroying freedom. We are forgetting key to life. We are forgetting that peace and freedom come from less law and not more. We are turning of "the people" into criminals. We must overturn the new laws. If we do not Cahokia will fall."

Hiamovi tried to maintain continuity during the transition that was now taking place. He attempted to maintain spirit and integrity among "the people". He attempted to hold the fabric of the nation together by continually instilling spiritual sobriety in all "the people".

It was the constant influx of refugees from all over the continent that put the strain on the resources of the land. The reserves of maze began to diminish. The hemp crop went uncultivated. The government found itself having to regulated the monetary system. Soon inflation began to tear the fabric of social structure which provided for all. "The people" began to coin money and provide allotments. Each was allotted according to his status. The system of allotments was the predicate to poverty and discontinuity. Resentment began to manifest itself in Cahokia.

It was the way of the Mongols to infiltrate any enemy with spies. Batachikan was fully aware that Mengwe had become dissatisfied and frustrated with their current status. He knew that if he could turn the Mengwe to the Great Mongol and against "the people" then the tide of the war could drastically changed. Up until this time the Mongols had formed no alliances with any of "the people". He knew that if he could bring the Mengwe into the fold of the Mongol Confederacy then the establishment of the Northern Horde would be well established. Batachikan began to devise his plan.

"In return for you allegiance we will allow the Mengwe to return to its lands and we will extend them in the east," said Batachikan.

"The Mengwe sware their alliance to the Great Khan of the Mongol Confederacy," Panowau of the Mengwe swore his alliance to the Great Mongol and to Batachikan's command. "My people will not fight against 'the people'."

"When we attack your people must not aid them in any way at all," ordered Batachikan.

"The Mengwe will not fight against you nor will we aid 'the people'," said Panowau.

"Then we have an accord, "said Batachikan finalizing the agreement. "We will need your help in breaching the city walls. Once the city is taken we will allow your people to leave Cahokia and reenter your lands as a part and parcel of the Mongol Confederacy."

"The people" continued to fortify the city. More people continued to arrive in to city. Soon crime and mayhem reared their ugly heads. There appeared a black market in almost everything of value. Prostitution began to be practiced among the refugees. Many people began to hunger. "The people" passed more laws and began to construct a prison and to exact harsher punishments.

"This way is not the way of the Olmec. It is the way of the Maya," said Hiawatha. "We are becoming as they became. We are supposed to be the peacemakers. Now we are becoming oppressors. The difference between the Olmec and the Maya was justice. That was their only difference."

The refugees were starting to feel pressure both inside and outside of Cahokia. They began to develop resentment toward "the people". "The people" thought themselves justified in the enactment of legislature which protected their integrity and sovereignty. Why was it unreasonable for "the people" to protect themselves and their homes? They thought.

Batachikan sent a final ultimatum to Hiamovi and "the people". His message made just one statement, "surrender or die". Then there appeared in the field on west of the Mississippi a host of more of more than a one million Mongol soldiers. On the eastern front the Vikings, Welsh, and Celts had managed to amass an army of two hundred thousand. They would squeeze "the people in" a vise.

"'The people' bow to none but the Great Spirit," was Hiamovi's only words in response.

The host and Horde of the Great Mongol camped at the gates of Cahokia.

"We are surrounded," Nosh said to Hiamovi.

"Our homeland is now death ground. There is but one choice when on death ground and that is to fight," Hiamovi responded.

With that Batachikan gave the order for an all-out assault on the land of "the people" and on their city. Within view on a distant field the Viking, Celts, and Welsh came forth to do battle. They were giant beings wielding giant weapons. The Celts came forth with stone axes the size of small boulders. "The people" unleashed a barrage of iron tip arrows at the line of the Celts. The giants fell in droves but did not relent. The each Celt was able to withstand three or four arrows before going down.

Batachikan gave the order for the Mongol army to make its push. Naran and Saran spasmed in their mirth before becoming very serious in their focus. This was what they had been waiting for. Now was the time to exact revenge on all who dare oppose the Great Mongol. Naran and Saran both held "the people" in great disdain. The two went forth with a purpose.

"Finally. Kill!" screamed Leif giving the order to attack.

"Take no prisoners," yelled Iggle signaling the army to march with a hand that was a few fingers short.

Word had gotten to the Berserkers that the assault was to begin. They came pouring down out of the northern territories of Aztalan like a plague and with a vengeance. Now everything became surreal. This was truly a world war taking place within the lands of Anahuac. Soldiers and warriors from the nations of the world who were either opposed or allies of the Great Mongol came to join the fight. The brother nations of the earth also came forth to fight for "the people".

The Mongol Horde had been switched on with no off button available. Tidasi and Heluska now formed a single army of two hundred thousand. The total warriors fighting for the cause of "the people" was estimated at more than two million strong.

The battle was engaged. There appeared three majors battles at once. The combined people's army of the west went forth to meet the Mongols. The Mongols began the assault. Naran and Saran were relentless as they moved through the army of warriors. The martial skill of the two and their army appeared to border on the magical. The Mongols enveloped the army of the west.

The astuteness of the Mongol at battle tactics bewildered and baffled the warriors. The warriors of "the people" saw the Mongols tactics as nebulous and obfuscated. The tactics that they employed gave the Mongol Horde an aura of mystery. The Missouri once again took the brunt of the attack. The Mongol had tried to subvert the Missouri as they did the Mengwe but were unable. The Missouri stood before the Great Horde with swords in hand. The Missouri were bolstered by new volunteers from the entire western half Anahuac and Kemanahuac. The battle raged in a bloody collage. In every way that was imaginable for men to die they died. The fighting went on day and night.

The Mongols employed their strategies of misdirection and faking out their opponents. They continual misled the Missouri counterattack into traps. Soon the Missouri found themselves chasing their own tail. And the Mongol eagerly cut off their head. After a bloody and intense battle the Missouri were defeated and scattered. Some Missouri did manage to make east across the river to the security of Cahokia.

Again it was the Chickasaw who stepped into the mix of the battle with Viking, Celts, and Welsh to turn the land bloody. One hundred thousand Chickasaw warriors routed the Golden Horde of the southeast. Once again the land was so bloody that no army could pass through it.

The Vikings ceded defeat to the Chickasaw and no more tried to enter in to their lands. The reputation of the Chickasaw spread even unto the ears of Batachikan. He was astonished that the Chickasaw could mount such an offense against the Golden Horde with inferior numbers. However, the Chickasaw would not campaign outside of their own newly acquired lands. They extended their boundaries in all directions and allowed none to trespass.

"The people's" battle with the Berserkers did not far as well that of the Chickasaw had. Their loss at the hands of the Berserkers was an all-out war in itself. The forces led by Tidasi and Heluska fought intensely against the Berserkers. Within a short time half of the warrior army had been killed. The Berserkers suffered heavily as well. Leif and Iggle would not be denied this time.

"Let's pray for a storm," Tidasi said to Heluska. Hoping that an electric storm would produce the pulse of four-million joules necessary to trigger the exploding wire and excite the red mercury causing the cascade effect and explosion needed to inundate the Michigan Valley."We must hold them here. We must destroy this army in its place."

Tidasi sent in wave after wave of warriors. They relentlessly attacked the Berserkers with impunity. All the warriors would give their lives if necessary to hold the Berserkers where they were.

"We will fight for our homes," said one the escapees from Berserkers prison camp. We will give our lives so that they will not advance to the south." The Berserker began to see that warriors of "the people" were continuing to fight as if there was no tomorrow.

The Berserkers were relentless and would only feigned retreat. At all times did they push toward the conquest of Cahokia. Tidasi and Heluska continued to fight against the Berserkers. The battle was a never ending engagement. Tidasi had forgotten that he was a man and fought as if he could not be killed. When he was observed from afar he appeared to be the manifestation destruction. He had made his intention to fight for the sake of fighting and to be killed in battle was the nature of war. Tidasi had come to realized that it was the way of the warrior to also walk on the road of death.

It was death that had now become the companion to all who entered the field. Even if they did not die on this particular day they now realized that death was sure to come, and that to want to live forever was inimical to the way of the warrior. Tidasi realized that it was those who cherished life who were the ones who were sure to die. He also realized that once all hope of life and living was abandoned on the battle field that one could find immortality. It was the immortality in death that kept the living alive. And to seek death in battle was the only true way for a warrior to live.

With sword in hand Tidasi and Heluska moved into the center of the field where it was most dangerous. Soon all the warriors had taken the field of battle in the center. The warriors had forgotten their own lives and become fearless. They had become fearless as the jaguar because they were now becoming aware of their own strength. The warriors now became the personification of cats catching rats, giant berserk rats.

The tide of battle was slowed but not averted. The name and reputation of the Berserkers was both well earned and well deserved. They would not be made to turn from their direction. More and more soldiers entered the field. The Batachikan had planned the logistics of the battle of Cahokia. The line of reinforcements and supplies seemed almost never ending. The war waged on.

Again the Berserkers made another surge into the defensive line of "the people". This time they beached the line. They had broken through. Tidasi realized that his warriors must not let the Berserkers reach Cahokia.

Tidasi stood in the middle of the field fighting for the life of his beloved country and city. He saw friends, relatives, and neighbors falling all around him. He saw that no matter how determined his army was they were simply no match in head to head conflict with the Berserkers. Again Tidasi ordered his warriors to retreat from the field. He reluctantly acquiesced to the inevitable. Once again the retreat was orderly. This time the retreat would back down the Mississippi to Cahokia.

The army now mounted a strategy of continuous harassment and forest warfare. They continued to hit the Berserkers from all angles. The warriors filled the forest with a multitude of traps. Every step toward Cahokia became tenuous for the Berserkers. And many found their ends by means of a trap laid by "the people".

Tidasi and Heluska had now become known to the Horde. A priority was set on killing them and eliminating the military genius that guided "the people". The two warriors become the most wanted heads in the Mongol Empire. Tidasi and Heluska continued to stand in the field and kill as many as they could. The fear of death still did not cause them to flee to a safe haven.

Chapter 16

"The people" drew in tightly to defend Cahokia and to make a last stand. They moved within the walls of the city. The entire economy of the land was disrupted and in ruins. The place of peace that had been the greatest city in Anahuac was now changed it seemed forever. The infrastructure of the city had completely given way to fear and aversion. "The people" of peace were now a people living in constant fear, distrust, and suspicion.

The mind that had kept "the people" unique in spite of mankind bowed to disruption. Divisions took place. "The people" became divided. The strategy of the Mongol psychology had been successful and was the greatest weapon in their arsenal was doubt. It had been the overstanding of "the people" with regard to all "the people" from different regions that made Anahuac what it was. The influence of the Horde in its divisiveness caused "the people" to begin to learn to hate where once they had loved.

"The people" began to think as they began to choose between giving and taking. They began to know the difference between love and hate. They began to see virtual differences in bloodlines. They saw the differences among those who lived within the city walls and those who on the outside. They began to view all foreigners suspiciously. "The people" became unhappy.

The gentle smile once worn by "the people" was no more. The continuity of the civilization was now lost. The government became corrupt. Hiamovi and Nosh attempted to give "the people" solace and hope. They attempted to remind them that it was faith that had built civilization. Hiamovi stood atop the Great Pyramid of Cahokia.

It stood in spite of the present troubles. It was evidence of the greatness of "the people".

Hiamovi stood surveying the city called Cahokia. Though now overcrowded the beauty of the city could not be covered. The well lit tree-lined avenues highlighted the beautiful architecture and the well laid grid of the city. Cahokia was planned city. It had not started as an encampment along the Mississippi. It had existed from the time just after the great flood. It had been built by the descendants of the Cushites, the Olmec. The domain of the Olmec encompassed all of Anahuac.

Though the landscape had not changed the aura surrounding the city had changed. Now "the people" had become mean. Resentment became paired with suspicion. "The people" went circumspectly around their city. Everyone became a suspect.

"Where is your identification. You are supposed to wear the marks of your nationality," said one of the security agents who represented "the people".

"I do not need identification. I am Mengwe," replied the man who was walking through area of the city designated as for the citizens only.

"You know the law. Only citizens may enter this area," said the officer. "Where are you going, Mengwe?"

"I am going to my family," said the man.

"Your family does not lived here, and you should not be here."

"I was taking the short way."

Soon more security arrived. The Mengwe man found himself surrounded by the hostile officers. They began to assault the lone Mengwe.

"We are going to teach you a lesson about trespassing into areas where you do not belong," said another of the officers. "Down on your knees."

"I have done nothing. I will not kneel," said the man.

"Do you defy us?"

"I have done nothing," the man repeated. "I have done nothing."

"Shut your mouth," said another angry officer.

The officers of Cahokia then began to beat the man. He attempted to run away. The faceless and nameless officers placed a copper wire around the neck of the man. They then began to punish him by beating him with clubs. The sound of the large clubs striking the bones of the man resounded with the shattering of his bones. They continued to beat him until all of his bones were broken.

Even after the man had been broken and shattered they continued to pummel him. They continued the thrashing of the man long after he had been killed. His body was then hang from the center pole of the sports field for all to see. The entire population was shocked and awed by the spectacle of the man hanging suspended by his feet. His lifeless and shattered body hung disjointed held together loosely by skin.

"Who is responsible for this," Hiamovi demanded of the council.

"It is our obligation to defend this land from all enemies both domestic and foreign. The Mengwe was in an unauthorized area. 'The people' must be protected," said Matawau, speaker of council.

"The Mengwe are the same as us. They are "the people" as we are. There is no difference," said Nosh.

"This day we are disgraced," said Hiamovi.

"We must take a strong stance with all the outsiders. Our way of life is threatened. We must defend our homeland," said Matawau.

"Why must we defend ourselves from the Mengwe?" continued Hiamovi.

"They now represent a threat," said Matawau.

"A threat in what way? They fight with us," said Nosh.

"The decision has been taken by a vote to which you were in attendance."

"This was not a unanimous vote taken to murder our brothers," said Hiamovi. "This vote was taking in order to ensure the tranquility of all 'the people' together."

A large crowd grew in front of the Great Pyramid. The Mengwe were incensed at the murder and mutilation of one of their own. This type of punishment had never been exercised against any before.

"You are all ordered go back to your quarters until further notice," shouted the commander of the security officers.

"Will you kill us all," shouted one of the Mengwe.

"Do not make this situation anymore difficult than it already is. Leave this place at once and return to you quarters," the commander shouted his order again.

"We want justice," the Mengwe began to shout in unison.

"Leave this place now," ordered the commander. "This is your final warning."

"No justice, no peace," shouted the Mengwe in unison.

The security officers poured into the field. They began to club the Mengwe mercilessly. The Mengwe now also took up arms. Soon a full fledged riot was taking place. Then there was a fire. Then there was another. The Mengwe began to burn everything. The security officers began to use deadly force. The first of many began to go down.

"The people" and Mengwe had always been brothers. They had come from the same origin. They had always known the same fate together. A member of the Mengwe was considered the same as "the people" until now. Now they were fighting to kill one another. Finally the Mengwe were subdued.

"We must speak with Panowau," said Hiamovi to Nosh.

Nosh made his way through field of disgrace that lay before him. Panowau stood silently and emotionless surveying what had been wrought against his people. He look deeply into the eyes of Nosh.

"What is it this that 'the people' have done? This day you have murdered your brother. How shall you ever redeem yourselves and be forgiven? How shall 'the people' stand before the One on the last day and explain this?"

"We have lost our way. We have done something that cannot be undone," Nosh said bearing the shame of "the people".

"What will you do now? Will 'the people' kill more?" asked Panowau.

"We want no fight. You have the words of Hiamovi and me that none of 'the people' will attack the Mengwe again," promised Nosh.

Batachikan saw from a distance the mayhem that was taking place in Cahokia. He ordered the assault to begin. The Mongols began to cross the Mississippi. The Vikings, Celts, and Welsh moved on the city from the east. And the Berserkers still battled the resistance from Tidasi and Heluska. Their way to Cahokia would not be so easy.

Batachikan chose this moment when the "the people" were com-

Whispers of a Man 159

pletely unprepared for the assault to launch his assault. They had become lost in their oppression of the Mengwe. The city came under siege. The security officers and the warriors who were protecting the city had been distracted by the violence of the riot and the insurgence. The fighting on banks of the Mississippi was ferocious and fierce. The foreigner warriors from the nations of the world now entered the battle against the swarming Horde.

Then the night sky became as day from the light of ten thousands flaming arrows which rained down upon the warriors who stood in the first ranks. Again and again the Mongols fired flaming arrows by the ten thousands. The army of "the people" employed the ballotechnic weapons. The Mongols went down in droves from the concussion of the blasts.

"Will you fight with us?" Nosh asked.

Panowau made no reply, turned, and walked away. Nosh turned toward the council chamber and Hiamovi. Panowau was now convinced that his decision to stand still while Cahokia was attacked was a correct one. It had been buttressed by the violent aggression of the security officers. The Mengwe warriors were ordered not to fight with "the people". The Celts began their assault from the east. The stone wielding giants came in columns toward the warriors who protected the way. The Welsh then swung around from the southeast in order to attack the rear of the army fighting the Mongols. The Vikings then pour down from the north.

Cahokia was squeezed in a triangle and the only escape route lay to the south. The fighting continued to rage with more than three million fighters battling at once. "The people" now stood on death ground. For them there was nowhere to go and the only recourse was to fight.

The Mongols breached the defenses on the bank of the river. Now they held a foothold and controlled the access to Cahokia by the river. They continued to moved to the east. There was hand to hand fighting taking place inside the city itself. The Mongols had sent soldiers to penetrate the line and the defenses. They coated the walls with very flammable pitch. The wood wall surrounding the city was set a blaze. Before long the burning wall caused more panic among "the people".

Hiamovi, Nosh, Matawau, and the council members remained with their elite guard inside the council chamber. Hiamovi and Nosh intended to force Matawau to turn from the course that he had set "the people" upon.

"The Mengwe are the least of our problems now," said Matawau.

"We have now lost our most important ally. This foolish action could cost us everything. Do you understand?" Hiamovi shouted at Matawau.

The Celts had entered the city by breaching the walls with their giant stone axes. They looked to smash everything that was within range. The stone axes that they swing were more like boulders shaped like axes. The Celts were not known for they diplomacy and keen intellect but more for their shear malevolence.

Soon the Mongols were also within the city walls. Naran, Saran, and Batachikan then appeared inside the walls. The two known as the Sun and the Moon tore through the security guards that stood before them. They could smell the sweat and sense the fear of those who stood guarding the homeland. They began to rend everything that lay in their wake. They raced toward the pyramid.

One-thousand elite guards of Hiamovi went forth to defend and meet Naran, Saran, and their soldiers. A pitch battle was taking place in Cahokia. Hiamovi and Nosh also took up their blades to do battle.

Naran and Saran cut a swath through the midst of the elite guard of Hiamovi. The elite guard came forward by the tens to meet the two, but even by the tens they were no match for the Sun and the Moon. They guards then attacked them by the hundreds. Naran and Saran picked up the intensity of their offense. The elite guard found that the answer did not lay in their numbers. A trail of bodies lay starting at the bottom of the pyramid and ascended to the top.

Matawau stood in shock as he saw the Mongols moving toward him. Fear gripped Matawau as he began to plead with the Mongols for his life.

"I surrender. I submit to the Great Khan," Matawau begged and pleaded.

The Mongols could not understand his language and did not acknowledge him in any way. He stood defenseless while Naran beheaded him on the spot where he ordered the Mengwe to be oppressed.

"You should have taken the offer of the Great Mongol," said Batachikan as he ascended the final step to the top of the pyramid. "Tonight I will sit on the throne of Cahokia and the banner of the Great Mongol will fly over your city."

"Not this night or any other night," said Hiamovi drawing his blades to the ready for action.

Hiamovi and Nosh moved forward to do battle with Batachikan and his guard. The blades were a blur as the fight began. Hiamovi moved forward toward Batachikan. Nosh moved against Batachikan's guard. The sound of blades clashing was echoed by the battle for Cahokia that was raging outside. Everywhere there was violence taking place.

Batachikan and Hiamovi fought with expert precision. The skill which Nosh possessed was not trivial. Nosh quickly dispatched a guard then moved toward the others. Nosh slew all of them with expert precision. He then joined Hiamovi against Batachikan. The two attacked the Mongol leader with impunity. They were determined to kill him. They attacked high and low. The Mongol general maneuvered in and out and up and down constantly changing levels. Batachikan had experienced many hundreds of duels. He had killed many. His swordsmanship was impeccable and defensive skills provided no openings for Hiamovi and Nosh to penetrate.

All around there was the sound of death everywhere. The Mengwe stood by watching as "the people" were slaughtered by the Mongols. The security officers attacked the Mongols by the hundreds and fell by the hundreds. The Celts continued crushing the heads of all that they came into contact with. With their giant stone axes they crushed "the people" to dust.

More warriors arrived to defend the city. Naran and Saran revealed themselves as the imps of violence that they were. The warriors moved forward to defend the great pyramid and the council chamber. Naran and Saran stood at the entrance to the council chamber to established ground zero and to challenge all that came forward.

Soon there were tens of thousands of Mongols within the city walls. Cahokia took on a surreal look as it became locked in an endless moment of endless war. From a distance the city was seen to be convulsing. It screamed in shock and pain as it avenues were turn into streams of blood and tears.

All the attention of "the people" was turned to the defense of the city. Tidasi and Heluska raced their war parties back to Cahokia. The Berserkers raced as well. The battle between the Berserkers and the warriors became hit and run all the way back to Cahokia. Now Cahokia was the true center of the world.

An eerie glow and smolder could be seen for hundreds of miles in the night. All who saw the glow of the fire felt the life that they had known slipping out of reach. The warriors ran faster to get back home. It was now as though they were running on a treadmill and getting nowhere. The Great Horde was now in its element, and that element was chaos and all-out war.

Hiamovi and Nosh continued to duel Batachikan who countered expertly. They two old warriors were on the offensive against Batachikan and it seemed that they were controlling the fight. Batachikan's double sword technique was something the two had not known. He moved in and out cycling in figure eight fashion of an endless circle bisecting the pyramid that they described with their tomahawks and blades.

Again and again Hiamovi and Nosh attacked high and low simultaneously. Again and again Batachikan countered their attacks. He moved as a timeless wind without limit or bounds. He then penetrated and ran his sword through the heart of Hiamovi.

"Ku Tu," screamed Nosh.

Hiamovi stood straight as Batachikan twisted his blade to ensure that he severed all connections of his heart to his body. He quickly removed the blade from the heart of the most important man in Cahokia without so much as giving it a second thought.

Nosh saw his lifelong friend fall dead before him. He had seen everything that he had known destroyed. He saw Hiamovi laying on the floor of the council chamber. Nosh suspended his head top, raised his spirit, and continued his assault on Batachikan. The two battled in endless barrages and volleys of deadly techniques.

Over and over the two attacked one another with the intention to annihilate. Nosh described the nine points of the pyramid while Batachikan describe the endless cycle of the figure eight. The two continued to fight into the night as the battle raged outside.

The bimibas that were situated in close proximity to the city continued to poured in. Then as the sun came up in the east the carnage and destruction of the night was exposed. The city had been burned to the ground. Only the structures made of stone were still standing. Bodies lay everywhere.

Most of the residences had fled during the night. The Mengwe had also left the city. Only the warriors and soldiers remained. Enapay and his bimiba had entered the field and were now moving toward sports field. There they found the Celts pounding everything they saw.

The bimibas formed themselves into war parties to make an assault. Enapay moved toward an extremely violent Celt soldier. His countenance became bigger than that of the Celt. Enapay began to issue out a thousand cuts to the soldier. The Celt stood in shock as he was cut up.

The other members of the bimiba became individual cyclones cutting everything Celtic in sight. Naran saw could see that a change had occurred in the field. He could see that it was Enapay who was weaving his way through the slow a foot Celts. Naran rushed the field. He remembered the defeat that he had suffered grappling at the hands of Enapay. Now he would take revenge against him for the humiliation.

Enapay could sense the aura of death and violence standing to his rear. He turn to see Naran standing waiting for his attention. Naran wanted Enapay to see his death coming. The two recognized that this was the fight that should take place now. Enapay and Naran moved hurriedly toward one another without a second thought.

Each enter into the personal space of the other. Enapay rolled beneath the parry of Naran sweeping from his feet with a kick. Naran rebounded from the earth with a bounce. Enapay rolled forward as a great river moving unceasingly toward Naran. His pyramid nine techniques were impeccable. He enjoined and engaged Naran continuously.

Naran seemed not the be greatly concerned with Enapay's assault on his life. He fought as though he wanted the fight to last forever. His curved sword circle in a perfect figure eight. Enapay found himself being attacked from all angles. He moved closer to Naran in order counter the long reach of the Mongol sword. The two fenced and parried continuously dueling. Naran found that the skill that Enapay possessed was formidable.

The armies of Tidasi and Heluska had now reached the city. The Berserkers were also reaching the field. The sight of the destruction of Cahokia was unbearable to Tidasi and Heluska. They both raced toward the great pyramid. The Mongol soldiers had taken possession of the Great Pyramid. The main battle still raged inside the council chamber.

Nosh moved like a cat about to catch a rat or a hawk about to catch a rabbit in his assault of Batachikan. He began to press the Mongol general. Batachikan began to lose the upper hand. Nosh who had traveled to the world and seen what had come of those who had gone before was not in awe of the Mongol. He continued none stop pressure on Batachikan. His tomahawk and blade ripped through the garments worn by Batachikan.

Batachikan was taken aback by the continual pressure and well-trained techniques of Nosh. Nosh pushed him more. Batachikan found himself tiring and losing the fight. Nosh came forward measuring Batachikan as he would the giant buffalo or giant deer.

Tidasi and Heluska were unaware that Hiamovi had fallen and that Nosh was battling Batachikan. Tidasi could see that Saran was still cutting a swath through warriors that were still coming. Tidasi and Heluska rushed the staircase leading to the top. They now cut a swath. Saran retreated inside the pyramid to aid Batachikan. Nosh had now disarmed Batachikan. The beaten general lay on the flood of the council chamber defenseless.

"You have come as a plague of locust to destroyed our land and our city. You have killed Hiamovi. Now you shall die," said Nosh to Batachikan as he prepared to deliver the final blow.

Saran dove in block the death blow that Nosh intended delivered to the head of Batachikan. Nosh moved forward to make the fight with Saran. Batachikan move safely out of harm's way. Nosh counterattacked with another strike to the person of Batachikan. Again

Whispers of a Man

Saran stepped in to parry the blow.

Now Nosh battled against two. He moved in on the two. He could hear and see everything. He had forgotten that he was alive and simply was. His skill and technique became tuned and his spirit was raised. Nosh felt no fear of death.

Tidasi finally reach the apex of the pyramid and the entrance to the council chamber. He saw his father engaged with the two Mongols. He moved forward to meet more fierce resistance inside the chamber from Mongol soldiers.

Batachikan and Saran now had regrouped their combined attacked on Nosh who continued to describe the pyramid by his technique. Again Nosh sought to take the heart of Batachikan. Saran moved into the forefront of the duel to protect. Nosh found himself pursuing Saran.

He began to rise above the abilities of Saran. Saran found himself at a deficit against Nosh. Nosh became the epitome of the dreams of "the people". He now fought his enemy for the sake of fighting. He was relentless. He moved in to kill Saran then to take Batachikan.

"You are the Moon? You should have brought the Sun with you this day," said Nosh as he prepared to cut the throat of Saran. "Today the Moon will be split into two."

Nosh brought his tomahawk and blade into position to take the head of Saran. Then there was a second that lasted too long. There was a flash of light that seemed too bright. There seemed to be an interruption of time somehow. And Nosh fell. Batachikan had run his sword through Nosh's back.

"No," said Tidasi as he entered the place where the battle was taking place. He had arrived in time to see his father fall.

Now the Berserkers, Celts, Welsh, Vikings, and Mongols filled Cahokia with the violence. There combined strength and power began to overwhelm "the people". Enapay and Naran continued to duel to the death on the center of the sports field. Enapay fought with the intensity of the jaguar. Naran fought with the claws and tenacity of an eagle.

Then Naran bisected the pyramid and ripped Enapay's stomach open with a cut. He then circled to continue cutting his throat. Enapay fell dead. Kitchi and Cheveyo saw their brother fall. There was now no recourse. Though the fighting raged the city was lost.

Heluska entered the council chamber and pulled Tidasi out as thousands of soldiers from the Mongols Hordes continued to enter Cahokia. Tidasi saw his father and Hiamovi laying dead on the floor of the chamber. He mowed his way forward determined to take Batachikan and Saran. His heart and soul did not want to let him retreat. Heluska forcefully removed his friend. Tidasi studied Batachikan and Saran. He knew that he could take their lives at the time. Heluska knew that Tidasi and the entire army would die if they did not retreat now.

The warriors of "the people" began their retreat. The doorway to the south was the only recourse. "The people" began to flee to the southeast and the southwest. Cahokia seemed to begin to convulse as they left. The Horde did not pursue the fleeing inhabitants as they abandon their home.

More and more soldiers of the Horde continued to inundate Cahokia. The demographics of the population change almost instantaneously. The violence turned to incredible carnage and genocide for those who were unfortunate enough not to have escaped.

The warriors who had been captured had their hands and feet cut off and thrown into pits. The women and children who were taken where made to dig large pits out of the earth that would be their graves. The women were made to enter the grave while they were still alive and the bodies of the dead and injured warriors were piled on top of them. The sound of the living could be heard as they clawed their way attempting to escape the horror of being buried alive in a mass grave.

The horror intensified as the Horde began to rape the women and children who had been taken. The strongest of "the people" who were able to survive were immediately enslaved. The dead appeared to be in an enviable condition. The tears flowed in torrents.

As the night came upon Cahokia the stench of death and the smoldering burn continued to permeate the air. Everything had been killed. The bodies of Hiamovi and Nosh were thrown down the long steps of the pyramid and dumped into massive open graves that had been dug out by the hands of "the people". The screams could still be heard as the last traces of warrior resistance within the city was eliminated.

All became silent as all eyes turned to the great pyramid. Naran and Saran stood at the entrance of the council chamber at the top of the pyramid. Batachikan made his appearance in the ceremonial dress of the Mongols. The red, green, and black traditional flag of "the people" was thrown down and the banner of the Great Mongol was raised.

All those who were present went down on one knee and bowed before Batachikan who was the surrogate and proxy of the Great Khan. Cahokia and Aztalan were now officially a part of the Mongol Confederacy.

The prisoners who were now slaves looked up to see Batachikan, and the Sun and the Moon standing over and above them. They looked up to see that their way of life was now finished. Many of them though they were experiencing this tragedy firsthand still could not believe what was taking place. They could not believe that "the people" of the most perfect disposition and harmony could overtaken by barbarians who ate their meat raw, who lived with dogs, and did not bath.

Though the fighting had been fierce "the people" knew that this happenstance could not have been a mistake of nature. Though they had followed the law of the One they still had fallen. This none could understand. Though buttressed by prayer and duty they were now a conquered people. The surrealism of this loss could not be fathomed. "The people" could not comprehend that they had lost everything in one fell swoop of the Mongol sword and bow. They saw that their civilization had been overrun by the Mongol sword and the Viking ax.

Batachikan knew what the others did not. He knew the destruction of "the people" was not the Mongol gain. In this war all had lost. He knew that the Mongols would not be able to resurrect Cahokia. He knew that the scar on the face of the land would take centuries to heal, and he also knew that the civilization would never be rebuilt.

That night all the soldiers from the Great Horde made merriment and mayhem. The games of terror and torture were turned up as the Horde became drunk on the wine and the blood of battle. Batachikan saw what had been wrought and knew that what he saw was not good. He knew that Nosh had been right. He and his army were like locust swarming, devouring, and leaving everything desolate in its wake.

He saw that what he had done and the work of his hands rendered him a barbarian. He had been particularly responsible for destruction of "the people" and of Cahokia. He knew that what had been done could not be undone.

"No more will those who call themselves 'the people' live in this place. We have removed them and replaced their wicked ways. Now they have been replaced by "the real people". This land is the Promised Land which was promised to us from the beginning by Odin. Now we have taking our rightful position as the rulers of the entire world. Though we were once rejected by man we are now the rulers of man. This land was the last bastion of the civilization of man. Now it is no more. So let "the real people" forever be written of and represented by the power and majesty of the eagle. And let those who once occupied this great land and who are now vanquished forevermore be recorded and describe as snakes."

With this one speech Batachikan rewrote the history of Anahuac and destroyed the legacy of "the people". He had issued out a story that would be retold as the story of the battle between the eagle and the snake. The symbol of land was officially change to the eagle.

Later in the night it began to rain. The thunder and lightning filled the air of the northern sky. It began to rain unlike it had rained anyone's memory. The thunder shook the earth and the lightning struck in fire and fierceness. All fell to the earth upon their faces. Fear and awe overtook them all. The thunder and lightning seem as thought it would never stop.

Then as if an iron thunderbolt had struck the Earth. A burning light and giant parasol appeared in the air. The sky became a bright as the day. A lighting bolt had struck the mountain of iron, copper, and uranium igniting the exploding wire. The exploding wire excited the superconductivity of the red mercury and caused a runaway cascading effect at the molecular level of the uranium. This was the cause of the first nuclear explosion in Anahuac since the war with Maya.

The narrow neck of the land which separated the northern sea from the Michigan Valley was rent asunder. The sea poured into the valley inundating everything with a deluge. All within the valley drowned in the mighty flood. The cities, pyramids, and mines of the valley all died quickly in what became the depths of the five newly formed great lakes. The stronghold of the Berserkers was buried beneath the newly release waters.

The air for thousands of miles in all directions became filled with fine dust particles. The lands of the north began to convulse and were broken into pieces. The temperature began to drop significantly. The season turn to winter again. It began to snow heavily. The ice began to return to the north closing the back door by which the Horde had come.

Chapter 17

The rain and snow continue fall on Cahokia. The spring had turned to winter and the summer did not come. "The people" sat desolate in the perpetual darkness that now enveloped the land. The blue sky had turned gray. The birds did not sign and trees did bud. The animals had suffered greatly in the war as well. "The people" did not find enough food to eat.

They began to eat anything that they could find to eat. They began to hunt the horse herds. It was the horses that were among the first of the animal species to become extent. Many species of birds also become extinct as a result of the war. The Anahuac elephant also vanished.

To the north five great lakes appeared to fill in the lush valleys that had once flourished. Thousands of communities, fertile lands, and most of the mining territories were now beneath these inland seas. The logistical supply line of the Great Mongol had been lost. Entire legions of Berserker and Viking soldiers drowned. This lost was devastating to the Mongol Confederation.

The Mongol state of Aztalan would have to be begun anew. The complete infrastructure would have to be rebuilt from the ground up. The Mongol Horde soon found themselves starving as well. They began to eat their horses, and before long there was not a single horse left in Anahuac.

Everything was now skewed and twisted out of shape. The Mongol Confederacy had succeeded in taking Cahokia, but at what cost. They had killed the land and "the people". The Horde had came, saw, and conquered. It was their motivation which was not readily apparent. The motivation for the invasion and attack on Anahuac and Cahokia was their unrelenting and unrequited desire to get back to their origin. They wanted to reenter humanity and become man again.

However, they could not reenter civilization and become man again. So like children mad with tantrum they destroyed it. They were incapable of overstanding and only capable of understanding so they never reach the heights. When they climb the staircase of the Great Pyramid of Cahokia they climb up to an empty city.

Batachikan surveyed the newest addition to the Great Mongol Confederacy. He saw dark clouds and felt the cold winds. It was he who had directly orchestrated the downfall of the last vestige of the beauty of humanity. He knew that he could not rebuild Cahokia so he continued to lay plans for the complete takeover of Anahuac. The Mongols then set about and began the desecration of the Cahokia.

Tidasi sat staring into nothingness and listened to sounds of emptiness. The emptiness that he felt was mirrored by "the people" as he looked upon them. His family had safely escaped with Kitchi and Cheveyo. Tallulah, Mona, Ayasha, and Elan were safe. "The people" were without means and only now had themselves. The women and children who had escaped were safe although most of the men had been lost.

The golden plates with the history of "the people" that had been written by Tehuti and given to Tidasi by Hiamovi were also brought away to safety by Tallulah. "The people" began searching for their family members. The tragedy of the loss had not set in with most of them. They were in mass shock and numb.

The mind of Tidasi replayed the sight of the death of Nosh at the hands of Batachikan over and over. He saw Enapay dying over and over at the hands of Naran. His pain was the pain of all and he knew their pain as well. He stood before "the people" to speak of what they must do.

"We are 'the people' who have lived in this land from the first. We are the indigenous people of this continent. Let there be no mistake about who came first. We have seen what our fathers and forefathers have built destroyed in a single day and night. The sweat of their brows fertilized the soil of the land, and the barbarians and relics of mankind have destroyed what we know."

"The people" began to here what Tidasi was saying to them. They became tuned to his words and knew that the war was not over and the fight had not ended.

"This war has cost us much but not everything. We are still here. To the north is what remains of the greatest city in all of Anahuac. We have lost many of our best men. We have lost Hiamovi and Nosh. I am the son of Nosh and I still live. And as long as I live Cahokia will not be forgotten. We must not allow our city to be desecrated by the barbarians from the north. We must return retake our city from them and push them back the in to sea."

The warriors reorganized themselves under the command of the Tidasi and Heluska. There were thousands of warriors waiting to move. First they would retake Cahokia then begin the war of insurgence that would be without end. Once again the war parties were decremented until five man bimibas were created. Tidasi took his youngest brother Kitchi into his bimiba. Cheveyo would move with Heluska's team.

Cahokia was in chaos. The barbarians could not fathom the significance of what they saw. Although Batachikan now sat on the throne he was not Ku Tu of Cahokia. He sat on the throne of a dead city. The Horde could not mirror was the symbiotic relationship that "the people" maintained with the Cahokia.

Anahuac was no longer the place of peace, but was now consumed with violence and booby traps. The casualties that the invaders took became a psychological burden. They sat in the dark, dank, cold of the wilderness. They began to take up living in cone shaped tents' called tepees. They simply found themselves unable to perform the necessary maintenance to live in the structures built by "the people". The Northern Horde were technologically incapable.

Everything wore an ominous aura and the average temperature dropped ten degrees. Anahuac become a cold and miserable place that was inhospitable to life. The dust generated by the nuclear explosion reflected the sunlight and warmth away from the surface of the Earth and caused global cooling and a mini-ice age.

"The people" became expert at infiltrating the defenses of the

Mongols. Cahokia became a very dangerous place. This severely impacted morale of the invaders. When they went out on frequent patrols they would return with fewer numbers than when they had started with. "The people" began to play with the psychology of the Horde. They began to lose their enthusiasm and loathe Cahokia, Aztalan, and Anahuac.

"By Odin, how much longer do we stay in this miserable place?" wondered Iggle.

"From the look of things we will see Valhalla before we see home," mused Leif.

"This war was supposed to be over in a few months and now it is endless. The snakes seem to be learning to enjoy it as some sort of a game. These hourly attacks of theirs are like clock work." said Iggle.

"War" became the occupation of the land. "The people" of peace had become the masters of brutality issuing out pain and misery. The warriors became the masters of stealth and subversion. They learned to disappear behind enemy lines then rise from the blackness of the abyss to become the Horde's worst nightmare.

The alchemist continued to develop weapon's technology. They found that rendering the fat of animals they could produce esters. These esters became the base ingredients of ballotechnic weapons. And by combining esters with petroleum they could produce a form of fire that could not be extinguished.

"The people" began a campaign of terror. They used fired as a primary weapon. "The people" had learned to develop low explosives, as well as, high. Each warrior was taught to make a type of hand-grenade from salt and sugar. Although these were low explosives they served to shock, blind, cause concussion to the enemy. The grenades performed exceptionally well in sending razor sharp shrapnel in all directions. This allowed the warriors to get close enough for a blade.

Exploding wire technology was developed as a trigger for igniting high explosive and generating energy for uranium amalgam bombs. However, these nuclear based weapons had been rarely used. The ecological impact of the Michigan Valley explosion was incalculable.

It was the fires that cause the Horde the most trepidation. The

Whispers of a Man 175

trepidation were such that few slept night. Petroleum could be found in large quantities in pools on the surface of the land. There was nearly an unlimited supply of oil and natural gas reserves which made these weapons practical.

In the still of the cold wet night the Tidasi would lead his army into the second battle of Cahokia. This was to be the battle for the spirit and soul the city, as well as, for its skeleton. Cahokia deserved a proper burial. Heluska moved his army to the flank of the Horde. The fields surrounding Cahokia and crisscrossing Aztalan was infused with the fuel for the endless fires and triggers for the previous laid copper wire. The significant addition to the technology was the refined nickel for the exploding wire triggers.

"They are magicians," Naran said to Batachikan.

"They are very clever. Their technology is the same as Egypt and Babylon. This civilization has built the world and we are destroying it," said Batachikan.

An emissary was sent from Tidasi to Batachikan. It was Kitchi whose bimiba that had been responsible during mission to inundate the Michigan Valley and had help to rescue the prisoners held by the Berserkers. He was allowed to enter the city and were brought before Batachikan. Kitchi looked to see Cahokia looted, sacked, and destroyed. He had also been roughed upped by the soldiers before being brought before Batachikan.

"Tidasi tells you that "the people" are tired of fighting. He says that this war has ruined our land and has killed many. We seek to end this war," Kitchi said.

This news came as a surprised to Batachikan. He never expected Tidasi to ask for a truce. A smile came to Batachikan's face for the first time in quite some time.

"Why did not you accept joining with us. We could have learned so much from you. Instead everything that they have accomplished will be forgotten. No one will know of the wonders that we have witnessed. One day no one will remember you and you shall called legends and stories. We shall always be remembered for what we have accomplished.

We have built the greatest society that the world has ever seen. We have given a home to those who you have cast out. What right do you have to bar us from the richness of life and civilization. Who are you to tell us that we are savage barbarians? You offer us the crumbs from your table and tell us to enter by the back door.

Unfortunately for you we are strong. Your days of arrogance are at an end. You think because you are ancestors of the first men you are entitled. You are entitled to nothing. Your Great Spirit is our Great Spirit. You have cast us out, but He has returned us to you as a test.

Cahokia is destroyed for this ignoble impulse. It is your haughtiness that has wrought your downfall. You think that you are superior and you are not. You pretend to be the most perfect of people but in reality your civilization is a failure. You have failed and everything that they believe in is a lie."

"We can see that you blame us because of your rebellious nature. We overstand everything you pretend to be true. Mankind was cast out because you are single dimensional. You lack compassion. This is your ignoble impulse. Your nature is of envy and deceit. You are the children of the world. You ancestors made a choice to follow an impetuous nature," replied Kitchi. "Man did not cast you out, but you cast yourselves out. It is your rebellious nature which makes you incorrigible. You call us snakes, but you speak with the forked tongue. We offered to share with you in trade and friendship. You are the liar and a wolf in sheep's clothing. You speak of the Great Spirit but you are spiritless. You are ghost who come to disturb the peace and bring war. Perhaps you are a test from the One, but not in the way that you think."

Kitchi then withdrew two grenades from his waistband and launch them in toward Batachikan. Batachikan dropped behind the curtain of his guards of whom most were killed. The concussion of the blast had been so close that it burst Batachikan's right ear drum and severely damaged the left. He was now almost completely deaf. Kitchi took off in the opposite direction disappearing in the confusion.

The blast was the signal to Tidasi to give the command to launch the counterattack on Cahokia. Hundreds of grenades filled the sky in a barrage and arrows fill it with fire that were launched into the city. Within a matter of minutes thousands of warriors entered the

Whispers of a Man

burning war torn city. The warriors of "the people" poured into the city in endless waves.

The Celts and Vikings had been ordered to guard the perimeter of the city. Fire continued to be the primary weapon of the warriors that was used against them. The sight of barbarians running in flames was everywhere. "The people" were merciless in the assault of the invaders.

Batachikan now could see as Hiamovi had seen. That being barricaded within the city was not necessarily a position of advantage. It could now be likened to a thief hold up in a house while outside waiting were the authorities. The Horde had failed to realize that it was not their way to capture and hold urban centers indefinitely.

And Cahokia was not a city that they could comprehend. This city like all cities that were built by the Cushites and their descendants had to be operated. The great pyramid itself was a machine which far beyond the comprehension of the Mongol Confederacy. The city the itself was a part of a symbiotic relationship with "the people". The Mongols and Vikings could not fathom the cities that were built by the builders of civilization. They had barely mastered the construction of log homes.

Tidasi attack the city that was his home with his army. He moved through the city knowing it intimately. This was the place where he had played with Heluska and his brothers as a child. His eyes sat upon the great pyramid. The warriors had become expert in stealth and had been able to penetrate the defenses of the Horde easily. Batachikan maintained his headquarters at the top of the Great Pyramid although he slept in his tent near his officers in the sports field. This area was securely controlled and he could sleep at least part of the night. The soldiers of the Horde stood to do battle again. Each weary soldier took up his weapon to fend off another assault.

Then there was an explosion at the foot of the staircase of the Great Pyramid. More explosions, fire, and smoke filled the field. The warriors were on the offensive. They were now reinforced from all of "the people" of Kemanahuac with the exception of the Mengwe. The warriors struck into heart of Cahokia like a thunderbolt.

This time it was not simply another probe or skirmish that the warriors were conducting. This was an all-out attack. The warriors were unrelenting and came from all direction by the thousands.

Heluska's army entered the city from the opposite side. The Horde found themselves this time squeezed in the deadly jaws of the vise of "the people". Tidasi and Heluska met and joined forces in the center of Cahokia. The war party of "the people" had taken the field en mass.

Cahokia again convulsed with the swarming violence. The blade was brandished and the tomahawk raised. The pyramid became ground zero and the pyramid nine techniques became the way. "The people" went on the offensive.

They enjoined the Celts with their large stone axes by inflicting a thousand cuts. They met the Vikings in tumultuous assault against their battle-axes, swords, and hammers. The Mongols found themselves being swarmed instead of swarming. The warriors of "the people" had propelled themselves as the dark skinned warriors of Anahuac against the northern Horde. "The people" could see a clear distinction between them and the invaders.

There were clearly distinctions that "the people" had come to realize. They began to draw distinctions of race. They saw the those who fought for the cause of "the people" could clearly be defined as Cushites and descendants of the same pyramid building civilization. And they saw that the invaders were descending from the those who were known as Gog and Magog, Vikings and Mongols. They were of those who legend had spoken of as having been banished behind the Caucasian Wall which lie between the Black and Caspian seas.

These lands were considered the northern void and no man's land. These dark and cold lands were regraded as the lands of the boogie man, and place were few returned if the ever entered. There were actually very few reports of men who had journeyed into the northern void with the exception of Tehuti. He it seemed was the great civilizer who had visited all nations, including the northern void.

This war had now become realized as a spiritual battle between light and darkness, and a war of good versus evil. "The people" began to see themselves as defending their homeland against the Typhonians. "The people" now understood that the Northerners including Mongols, Vikings, Celts, Welsh, and Indo-Asian-Europeans were of the same origin. These were the descendants of the those who had been banished from civilization so long ago and were now re-emerging as the manifestation of darkness.

Now "the people" realized why they had been attacked. The Horde did not want to trade or union. They wanted the completed destruction of the Cushite civilization that had giving birth to them. The Horde had been infused with a recessive gene at their creation and were in capable of joining or rejoining man in civilization.

Naran and Saran entered the field against Tidasi and Heluska. Cheveyo, Kitchi, Bodaway, Elsu, and all of the thousands of other unnamed warriors who stood together. The battle was joined. Arrows and swords ripped their way to their targets, and tomahawks and blades sliced. Tidasi locked his attention on Saran with unrelenting intensity. Heluska set his attention on Naran. The four twisted in and out of space winding their way through the field.

The tall bronze frame of Tidasi stood powerfully before Saran, who had been responsible for killing Nosh and Hiamovi. Saran open with his own assault of arrows. Tidasi did not whence as plucked the arrows out of the air with his blade. He moved directly toward Saran. Saran did not retreat. He moved forward as well with his sword cutting through the air while he described the figure eight. His curved sword did not discriminate as he cut.

Tidasi and Saran engaged one another and did not separate. Tidasi was able to get close without being cut. He embraced Saran tightly before body locking him and tossing him through the air like a doll. He following Saran with his blade and tomahawk prepare to deliver a cut.

Heluska and Naran battled close by in a violent assault. Heluska moved close to Naran and never allowed the Mongol to open any distance. Naran's sword ripped through the air cutting the stomach of Heluska. His stomach was cut it but was not fatal.

Heluska continued his pursuit of Naran. His blades maneuvered through the cycle of the figure eight. He brought his tomahawk into the right side of Naran perforating his liver. Naran looked down to see the mixture of bile and blood coming from his side.

Tidasi and Saran continued in their life and death battle. Tidasi circled cutting in two the right biceps of Saran then continuing circling while describing a pyramid into his body. Saran began to feel the gaps between his skin and his bones. Tidasi began to fillet him. Saran stood bleeding and one armed.

"You killed my father, who was a real man. When you stand before me you are nothing. Before you die know that my father was Nosh of 'the people', and that his wife will know that her husband was avenged," Tidasi told Saran.

"We shall see snake," Saran refused to believe that he could be beaten.

Saran raised his sword to continue to fight. His fight became more violent in his reprisal against Tidasi. Tidasi moved in stillness and he moved before Saran tired to move. Saran found himself unsteady in his offensive against Tidasi.

Heluska continued to inflict Naran with tomahawk chops to his vital organs. Naran continued to struggle with his strength failing. Heluska could see that Naran was becoming disoriented. He moved in closer and chopped of the top of Naran's head off with a single blow. Naran died while he was still standing. Heluska delivered a very powerful thrust kick to that sent Naran back down into one of the trenches that had been prepared for dead.

Tidasi wound himself around Saran cutting his muscles from his bones. Then Tidasi bisected his other biceps. Saran was unable to hold his weapons. Tidasi moved in and locked Saran again in a reverse body lock send crashing down on his own head. Saran lay in the dirt defeated and dying. Tidasi stood over him, then, mounted him with blade in hand.

"I am Tidasi the son of Nosh and the friend of Hiamovi. Today I will take your heart and present it to 'the people' for the loss of two great men," Tidasi spoke his words to Saran.

He brought his blade down into the chest of Saran. Saran was still alive when Tidasi cut his heart from his body and held it up for him to see. Saran opened his mouth to speak and died. The Sun and the Moon lay dead in to soil of Cahokia. Naran and Saran had seen a thousand campaigns in distant lands. Now their legend was finished in a distant land in the city called Cahokia.

The warriors freed the captives that the Horde had held. The strong among them remained to join the fight and immediately took up weapons to fight the enemy. The numbers continued to mount against the invaders. The ex-prisoners were a reliable sources of information.

"The people" counterattack was not unexpected, but the intensity of the attacked was heightened and charged. The Celts, Welsh, and the Vikings were routed in the this battle. The Mongol Army sustained heavy losses. The Horde led by Batachikan abandoned the city. They were moving east to consolidate their hold on the land. They had kept their agreement with the Mengwe so far and found no threat from them.

Tidasi with Heluska, Cheveyo, and Kitchi once again stood atop staircase of the Great Pyramid of Cahokia. That did not take away the pain of the loss that they felt. All that they saw were the ruins that were left. Tidasi entered the area where the longhouse of his family had once stood which was now gone. He saw a toy that had belonged to Elan. He put the toy into the bag that he carried.

Chapter 18

The battles continued to be waged. The day had now become endless night. The battle for Aztalan had become an endless war. Cahokia was taken, retaken, taken, and retaken again. The months turned to years. Warrior-ship became the major occupation of all the men of Anahuac, and it became the sole occupation of many. The war became generational.

Tidasi's son Elan was now a warrior of "the people" and had grown in prowess and valor. He moved with the others who were now outstanding fighters and warriors. Heluska had also seen his sons grew into and become warriors as well. In fact all the sons became the next generation of fighters.

The warriors continued to fight a war of insurgency against the Horde. The intensity of the battles grew at each encounter. The warriors of "the people" became adept at unrelenting attack and sudden disappearance. The were also become expert in the use of ballotechnics. The manufacture of weapons of mass destruction became the primary industry of Anahuac and "the people".

Now it was readily acknowledge by all that the nuclear explosion that had inundated the Michigan Valley and caused the formation of The Great Lakes was the turning point of the war. The explosion had caused a global cooling that seemed that would never end. The inundation and deep freeze had immediately caused the destruction two thirds of the Horde Army and all those who were en camped in Michigan and Wisconsin. The invaders were beginning to lose the taste for war with "the people". The young had seen themselves growing old in this war.

"What the hell are we still doing in this godforsaken place," said Iggle, who was a few fingers short and still in Anahuac after all these years.

"We going to die in this place," said Leif, who also wore many scares from the many battles.

The two now old soldiers had participated in more than one hundred battles in Aztalan, including four at Cahokia. They had also seen many of their comrades killed. They had seen the Berserkers decimated by the warriors over the years. Most of the soldiers had settled, took to farming, and raising families.

These Northerners who had come as invaders had fallen in enamored with the land. They built extensive settlements and cities throughout the northeast. Now the war was coming to them.

"If only I could see Caucasia once more I would never leave," said Iggle motioning with his fingerless hand.

"I just want settle down with my dog," said Leif. "We get one more chance to finish these snakes."

"Well let's get it over with," replied Iggle.

"The people" continued to view Aztalan in the same way. They were defending their homeland from invaders, and they would never end their struggle to rid the land of them. War became a part of their psyche. They began to live for the fight. To die in battle was better than to live as a conquered people. "The people" continued to wage endlessly against the Mongols and Vikings and never thought of peace.

Batachikan found that desertions were becoming commonplace. Many of the soldiers who grew tired of the fighting moved to the west and settled with other refugees. Soon new tribes began appear and live a nomadic lifestyle. Some of Celts and the Welsh went on the to begin a tribe called the Mandan. Animosity between "the people" and "the real people" as the Horde took to calling themselves began to become meaningless. The taste for blood was losing its savor.

Batachikan sent messengers to Tidasi to negotiate a truce. Tidasi cut their throats. Batachikan had grown far apart from the Great Khan although he continued to send tribute back home. It seemed that the Mongol Confederation was having the internal problems that happened when a bureaucracy grew too big. This war had been too

Whispers of a Man

costly in terms of money and men. Batachikan maintained his post and continued to command the army with strict Mongol discipline.

"Their will be no peace until each pale devil is removed from this land," Tidasi told the messenger before he dispatched him.

"The people" instituted a policy of not taking prisoners. This tactic appalled the Batachikan. Tidasi and "the people" become associated with only violence and terror. The Horde began to paint a picture of Tidasi as a terrorist and began to associate negativity with his dark skin.

The invaders began to tell stories of the dark skinned monster who would come and take the children in the night. Tidasi became stuff of their nightmares. They associate all things of brutality, pain, and misery with him. Though he was fighting to regain his home from these northern invaders he became known as "king of the snakes". The snake was demonized by the Horde.

Batachikan realized that the only way to end this war was to destroy "the people" once and for all. Tidasi also realized there was to be no sharing of the land and no negotiations. He ordered all the war parties to advance toward the Horde stronghold in the northeast as a single army.

Tidasi had now become the picture of his father Nosh. He was a true man of Aztalan. He had killed many and had seen many friends and family members die as well. He and all the other warriors vowed that there would never be peace with the Horde. The Viking and Mongols became known by their looks.

Any permanent settlements that the Horde built was attacked. They did build more permanent settlements east of the great lakes in Canada. The Mengwe were not so comfortable with Horde as neighbors. Tidasi would pursue the Mongols and Vikings into the Ethiopian ocean if that was necessary.

The Mongols and Vikings had built a society in the north and east of the great lakes. They called their state Cumorah. The state was in a region of resources, minerals, and other abundances. This area was obviously a source of tremendous wealth. The land and climate was suitable. The Horde in Anahuac was concentrated here. Now they had something to lose. Something that they valued very much. There was now a generation of them who were born in Anahuac.

They were beginning to call Anahuac home.

"Their army is camped at the foot of a hill in a place called Cumorah. They have built many cities in the north and there are many women and children," Heluska informed Tidasi.

Tidasi ordered his army to move on Cumorah. His army was now a seasoned as the Horde. The mention of the approach of the warriors of "the people" brought fear to the hearts of the new settlers. Both armies gathered in the valley at the foot of a mountain.

Each army was fully equipped with the latest weapons. They carried carbon steel swords and shields. These new weapons were both stronger and more light weight. This gave the Horde a significant leap forward in the agility and tactics of their soldiers. They had found that in most encounters that they had been slower to a man than the warriors.

"That is where we shall meet them. We are going to end this war and push them into the sea. They shall never know peace in our land," Tidasi replied to Heluska. "Order the army to prepare for the battle. Today is the day that we have been fighting for."

It was cold as usual on the day that the two vast armies faced each other in the Valley of Cumorah. "The people" had developed a military system in a relatively short time. They had learned to employ flags and banners as coordination and signaling devices in addition to the smoke and drums. Most of the highly technological expertise had come into disuse due to the loss of the knowledge that had come with continuous war.

This day, however, was one of those rare days when something decisive would take place on world stage. This day someone would win this war and someone would lose it. This was the battle to end all battles.

All the soldiers and warriors entered the field. Batachikan stood at the head of his army. This was the day that he had waiting for all these years for. This was the day when his own personal battle would be completed. He had long hoped that he would be able to stand at the last battle with his sword in his hand.

All the old soldiers were present. Leif and Iggle though now old still held the Viking passions for mayhem and despised the life of the farmer that they had adopted. Though few of the original soldiers of the Vikings and Berserkers were left Leif and Iggle were still around. They relished the opportunity to die on the battle field.

The population of the Horde had grown significantly due to amalgamation with the indigenous people, including the Mengwe. The Mengwe had maintained their truce with the Great Mongol and were returning to relative prosperity.

In the seconds before the battle was to begin Tidasi look at his friend Heluska who stood next to him as always. He turned to his left to see his brother's Cheveyo and Kitchi. He turned again to the right and saw his son Elan standing also beside him.

"Bring the tablets forward," he ordered the bearer. "Elan, this is the record of 'the people'. They must not be lost. If I fall you must preserve this record. This is the record of 'the people' written in our language and tells of our story here in this land that is our home. The story of the great city of Cahokia must not die and must live on forever. By the end of this day this war will be over. If I fall you will lead our people to another place in the south. I give to you these tablets as Hiamovi gave them to me. Now take these tablets do not let them fall in to the hand of our enemies."

Elan took the tablets with honor from his father and returned to his place in the ranks. Tidasi looked again at Heluska and smiled. They both knew that this day they would free Aztalan from the Mongol and Viking invaders.

"Forward," Tidasi gave the command to advance.

"Forward," Batachikan also gave the command to enter into the decisive battle.

The two armies rush toward one another with the same intention. This day there was no place for fear in the field. Fear itself could not find a place in the ranks. The battle was on.

Tidasi set his gaze upon Batachikan like a hawk upon a bird. He singled him out like a bird in the midst of a flock. His sight did not stray from his prey. He had now waited many years for the chance to avenge Hiamovi and Nosh. The memory of Batachikan running his sword through the back of Nosh replayed itself in Tidasi's mind over and over again.

"Tidasi," said Batachikan brandishing his sword.

Tidasi said nothing as he enter the area of Batachikan's space.

Two entered into mortal battle. The swordsmanship of Batachikan was as always impeccable. He brought with him into the field no expectations of living or dying. He was a soldier who had become a warrior and had given up his life long ago when he had been first sent away from Cahokia empty handed.

The two generals fought with destructive intentions. Tidasi still brandished the blade and tomahawk. His pyramid nine techniques were well-trained as they had always been. He moved through the midst of circling double edge swords. Bowing under the slash of Batachikan he cut the tendon behind his right knee.

Batachikan continued to fight his fight. His eyes and the intention of his swords never left Tidasi. Though bleeding and on one foot his continued to struggle. Tidasi again attacked Batachikan with impunity. This time Batachikan defended and ripped across Tidasi's abdomen. Tidasi drop to his knees from the severity of the cut.

"Tidasi, today you shall join your father," Batachikan said as he prepared to finish Tidasi.

Batachikan moved to take the head to Tidasi. This time Tidasi went high instead of low and brought his tomahawk through the left side of Batachikan head. Batachikan dropped to his knees. Tidasi wrapped himself around Batachikan with his leg lock coiled tightly so that there was no escape and whispered into the ear which still had hearing.

"I am Tidasi of 'the people', the original people of this land. I am the son of Nosh and the friend of Hiamovi. This day I shall take your heart from your body while you are still alive. No that it shall be presented to "the people" as proof that we have revenged our fathers, brothers, and sons which you have taken. Your heart shall burn in the sacred alter of Cahokia which you have destroyed. Know this day that "the people" have fought against you and prevailed."

Tidasi then wound himself tighter around Batachikan until the sound of his bones cracking could be heard. Then he mounted him and plunged his knife into his chest. He severed the arteries connecting his heart to his body with the same blade with which he had killed Saran. He reached into the chest of Batachikan, and pulled his beating heart out of his body and held it before him. Batachikan looked at his own beating heart in the hands of Tidasi. At that mo-

Whispers of a Man

ment Batachikan could hear the sound of a flute. He could hear the same peace giving sound that he had heard so long ago. At that moment peace descended upon him and he died.

A Mongol sword entered through Tidasi back and he fell on top of Batachikan. The battle of Cumorah was the longest, bloodiest, and greatest battle of "The Greatest War". More than a million soldiers and warriors died en masse. The loses that day for the Horde was insurmountable.

"Tidasi," Heluska called to his friend, "You cannot died today my brother."

"I am just resting," the injured and weak warrior said to his friend with a smile. "Help me to my feet."

Tidasi stood up to see that the battle was done. He saw Cheveyo, Kitchi, and Elan were there. Birds circled overhead preparing to feast on the dinner table of carnage that was set. The warriors had defeated the Horde Army. And the remainder of the Horde was routed and retreated to the shores of the east coast of Anahuac.

"I am for one happy to leave this hell on Earth," said Iggle. "I am not ready to go drinking in Valhalla."

"Yes, I never liked this stinking place anyway. It's just much too hot. This damn sun just burns my skin," agreed Leif. "I would rather vacation in Caucasia in the cold ice than spend another day here. And good riddance to 'the people'."

With that the last of the Vikings began to leave Anahuac and Aztalan never to return again. "The people" burned and exploded everything that reminded them of the barbarians whose origins were in central Asia.

The Mongols found it more difficult to leave the land that they had invaded. The back door was closed by glaciers and there was simply nowhere for them to go. They moved into the east coastal area of Anahuac and set up tribal communities that were ever hostile.

The Mongol command structured became fragmented after the death of Batachikan. The infrastructure disintegrated although the Mongols continued to call themselves "the real people". They had changed the face of the continent forever. The did set up a new confederation in the Delaware area of the east which had been a Viking stronghold.

Chapter 19

Cheveyo, Kitchi, and Elan each led a group of "the people" to new homes within Anahuac. They would live far from the descendants of the invaders who now called themselves "the real people". The war was never officially ended and hostility would always remain between the two peoples. Tidasi continued to fight and train warriors to fight the endless war and Heluska remained with him fighting on. The fighting continued on for generation after generation.

Elan led "the people" to the southeast into Tennessee and Carolina where they built a new nation. Kitchi and Cheveyo led their groups of "the people" to the south and southwest. They also built new nations.

Cahokia never return to its previous glory because it could not recover from wounds and scares of "The Greatest War". Many impostors entered the abandoned city claiming to be the builders though they had no idea of the prestige and majesty that once was Cahokia. They were completely unaware of the technology which was the foundation of the city. Cahokia became a lost jewel which lay in plain view.

The city eventual fell from memory and into decayed. As the years past the city became overgrown with vegetation and cover by dust and soil. The Great Pyramid of Cahokia eventually took on the look of an out place mountain in the plains of southern Illinois. The other buildings within Cahokia were also covered and over grown.

The civilization that had once spanned an entire continent was now gone and a thing of the past. The miraculous technology became the tales that were told to children as stories of fantasy. Soon "the people", the Mengwe, and "the real people" forgot the roles that they had played in "The Greatest War" that ever was.

The great civilization became a fraction and reflection of its former self. "The people" began to focus once again on nature and living in harmony as they once had. They were still the most advance nation of Anahuac but they had fallen far below the level where they were before the war. They did build new cities.

"The people" and the Mengwe never return to the friendship and harmony that they had known from before. The two groups of the same family came to view one another with enmity even as they forgot the past. The Mengwe also never fully embraced the "the real people" as true friends although a tenuous peace persisted. They maintained tight borders with each other. Eventually they became enemies.

Following the war there was a disconnect between the nations of Anahuac. The nations west of the Mississippi had been practically wiped out by the war. There had been massive destruction by detonation of ultrahigh explosives which forced inhabitants to live as cliff dwellers. The entire southwest region had been convulsed and turned into a desert. The fauna and ecosystem of the southwest was swept away. The climate of the region had also been change dramatically. The rain stopped.

The devastation of the war did not confine itself to "the people" but touched all life. Many animal species became extinct or decimated. The giant short-faced bear, giant deer, and giant buffalo were gone. The pygmy elephant, horse, and numerous other animals were swept away from the face of the land and were never seen again. Countless birds also disappeared from the scene.

The nations of the world also lost the knowledge of Cahokia, Aztalan, and Anahuac. They had lost remembrance for the same reasons as everyone else had, the Mongol Confederacy and Northern Horde. The Horde which had originated in Caucasia had wiped the slate clean. They had destroyed all things and crushed civilization.

This marked the end of the Cushite civilization that had once consisted of forty-five kingdoms which had encompassed the entire planet. The Cushite civilization was not just the brown skinned civilization of east Africa, but was the civilization that had begun when

Zep Tepi had resurrected it following the great flood.

Chapter 20

Rat and Duute had been sitting spellbound the entire time that Mister Johnson had told the story of "The Greatest War. The sight of the two children sitting with their mouth's wide open brought a chuckle to Mister Johnson.

"That is the story of this land that we call America now. That is the story of "the people" who are called Mulattoes, Colored, and other names which were given to them during the period of slavery and who have always been in this land," he continued.

"What happened to Tidasi and his wife," asked Rat.

"Tidasi never stopped fighting. Some things are worth fighting for. His wife moved with "the people". He got home to see them when he could. His folks settled about round these parts."

"I knew it," said Rat.

"This all happen more than a thousand years ago and of course they are all gone now," Mister Johnson said.

"They are not gone. They are still living in us," said Duute.

"That is right. In us," said Mister Johnson.

"Yes, 'the people' tried rebuild a new civilization. Of course after a while the folks from Europe come again and this is where we are today. So most of 'the people' are lost now and do not know what to think," said Mister Johnson.

"Or where they come from," said Rat.

"I am not lost," said little Duute.

"We are found now," said Rat.

"Yes, you are right. We are found now," Mister Johnson said with a laugh.

The rain stopped and the sun started to peek out from behind the clouds. The rain washed air smelled so good. The birds started to sing.

"What happened to Elan and Ayasha?" asked Rat.

"They lived with Tidasi and Tallulah in their new home round about these parts."

"You mean they moved here to Beasleytown?" asked Duute.

"Not just Beasleytown but almost the entire southeast, like the Carolinas, Tennessee, and Virginia. They needed a big country for a big people."

"Did they ever find peace again?" asked Rat.

"They rebuilt and lived in harmony for a while, but the still never became friends with the "the real people". And when the white folks came back from Europe about five hundred years later they had forgotten everything and everybody. Many of the folks that they called 'Indians' were their relatives."

"Relatives," said the wide eyed Rat.

"Yes, relatives because white folks all came from the same place. They come from the same source. All the those Vikings who came here before were the ancestors of the some of the those Indians, especially the "the real people" and other northern Indians. It was a real surprise when "the real people' saw their long lost returning cousins did not remember them. On the day that the Vikings were run out they promise to return with reinforcements. They never came back."

"So when they did come back they didn't remember their own people," said Rat.

"The first thing that they did was invade and take they land from them. Then they gave then all kinds of disease and plagues. And finally they made them walk two thirds across the country to Oklahoma. And you know what?"

"What?" Duute asked quickly.

"When they got to Oklahoma guess who they met?" posed Mister Johnson to the children.

"Who?" asked Rat.

"The descendants of 'the people' and all the those people who they had fought to take the land from. The United States govern-

Whispers of a Man 197

ment had forced "the people" and "the real people" to live together. Suddenly those old enemies had to become friends and learn to live together. Except now they live under the rule of the mankind. This what you call ironic," Mister Johnson laughed.

"Ironic," Duute repeated the new word.

"That means that the last laugh was on them," explained Rat.

Mister Johnson and the children just looked out into the field and wonder what it was like to walked the long avenues and to see the Great Pyramid of Cahokia glistening. They mused about the freedom that "the people" had once enjoyed. They could even see the fields full of "the people" playing games.

"Yes, eventually all 'the people' were forced to live and work together. By the time that they had realized that living together was the way it was too late. By the time they realized that you just cannot come to take something from someone everything was lost. You just cannot say that millions of people do not and never existed," Mister Johnson went on.

"Like the white folks. They did the same thing." Came the words out of the eight-year old mouth.

"Yes, it is like history repeated itself. Except the was no great nation for them to destroyed. It was gone before they got here. Even though it was their ancestors who destroyed it the first time."

Again Mister Johnson saw the irony of it all. He knew that it was the Europeans who had returned with a no memory of the past. He also new that history was repeating itself. When he looked out into that field. He new that those days would never return.

"Rat...Duute," the voice of a woman could be heard in the distance.

"It's momma," said Rat.

"Momma," said Duute.

"I was worried to death. Thank God you children are okay," said Amanda embracing and kissing the children.

"We were with Mister Johnson. He told us all about Cahokia," said Rat.

"And 'the people'," said Duute.

"Did he? Well you two will have to tell me all about it. It sounds like a very exciting story," Amanda said. "First we are going to talk about how you two cut Dump's top-knot and put a blacksnake down Leroy shirt while he was sleeping."

They were caught again. Both of the wore the looks of the guilty. All that they could do was admit it.

"We're sorry," apologized Rat and Duute.

"Let's say good-bye to Mister Johnson for today."

"Good-bye Mister Johnson," the children said together.

Mister Johnson just sat and smiled looking out into the field and said, "Now if you listen real close you can here sound of the flute being carried on the wind. And when you listen you have to listen real close because it ain't just a sound being carried. It is also the sound of man. What you are hearing are the whispers of a man."

Chapter 21

She held her sons in her arms on a cold winter's night. The sun set early these days. The woman had grown from a child in Virginia and migrated to the north like most the Southerners from the farms in search of work in the cities.

"It sure is cold today," she said to her sons.

"I am not cold momma," said her oldest son.

"I got to make dinner cause your uncle Duute is coming to visit."

"Uncle Duute," said the youngest.

"He is coming all the way from Virginia to visit us here in Detroit. Your uncle has traveled around the world and now he is coming to see us. Then we are going to take a trip to Cahokia."

"All of us?" asked, the older of the boys, Assad.

"Yes, your father, Elan, you, me, and uncle Duute and his family."

"I am going to travel to when I grow up."

"I know, Assad. That is what all the men of our family do. They always travel the world to see everything that people built long ago, and then they come back to tell."

"I am going to travel too," said the younger of the boys.

The knock on the door had that certain beat that the woman recognized. She, Assad, and Elan ran to the door. They were so excited that they could hardly contain themselves.

"Duute."

"Rat," said Duute, now a man, embrace his sister who he had not seen since before his travels.

"Uncle Duute," Assad happily jumped into the arms of his uncle.

"You are growing very fast, Assad. Is that Elan?"

"Hi uncle Duute."

"Elan, this is Ayasha my daughter and your cousin," Duute introduced the children for the first time."

"Assad and Elan, I brought you some books," Duute gave the books to his nephews. "These are books that I made just for you two. They are picture books from all the places that I have visited in my travels. There is one place that not in them?"

"What's that uncle Duute?" asked Assad.

"Cahokia. And were are going to go there and see it ourselves. Because that is the place where "the people", our people come from."

Assad and Elan studied the books full of pictures of all the things that were built by those who had gone before. They studied the pictures of pyramids that Duute had taken from places that he had visited all over the Earth. Their minds became filled with wonder as they studied the photographs carefully.

The next day the they all stood at the foot of the Great Pyramid of Cahokia.

"Is this the place were 'the people' lived?" asked Assad.

"I want to lived here," said little Ayasha.

"Me, too," said Elan.

Rat and Duute smiled at each other. They had promised each other that they would name their children after Elan and Ayasha, the children in the story that Mister Johnson had told them so many years ago.

"That is Cahokia where 'the people' of the most perfect harmony lived," said Duute.

Rat and Duute had vivid memories of the story that Mister Johnson had told them. They could hear the sounds and sense the life that was. They knew that in the place where they now stood there had once been a magnificent city. In this place had lived an amazing people in whose spirit was the maintenance of the destiny of a nation and civilization.

Assad, Elan, and Ayasha like their parents when they first heard of Cahokia stood marveling at the impressions that were still left in the land after a thousand years. They thought that they could also hear the sounds and see the sights of Cahokia.

"I will visit all these places like you and I will tell the story of 'the people' too," said Assad.

"Me, too," said Elan.

"And me," agreed Ayasha.

"First you have to study," said his mother.

"I am going to read all the books in the library," Assad promised.

"Me, too," Elan also promised.

"And me," said Ayasha.

"I am going to hold you all to that," said Duute.

They climbed, stood, and looked on top of the mountain that was once The Great Pyramid of Cahokia. Then Rat and Duute began to tell the story of Cahokia and the Olmec civilization. They told the children the story of man and how their family had always live in this land. They also told the children many would call them and identify them with names and places which had nothing to do with nationality or heritage.

They told them that they should always remember that they were the indigenous people of this land. They told them that if anyone should ever ask them about their race, nationality, or heritage that they should simply tell that person that "I am not Mulattoe, Colored, Negro, Black, or any other name. I am of "the people".

Epilogue

The great state of Virginia had outlawed the existence of Indians in the state long ago. So Indians were unknown and unseen in Virginia, Maryland, and most other eastern states. The term "Indian" was the term that the conquerors had given to 'the people" who they had found occupying the land that they coveted.

Indians, Mulattoes, Negroes, Coloreds, Freemen, Black, and African-American were all words describing the same people. They described the dispossessed and disenfranchised. The "Indians" that were forced to amalgamate eventually became intermixed Europeans, Africans, and others.

The knowledge of the past and of self was lost. The law was destroyed and lost as well. The language and culture was stripped. The religion was destroyed. "The people" soon lost any sense of the greatness that their ancestors had once known. They began to believe that they did not originate in the land where they had been born.

"They people" began to believe that they had no right to they land in which they lived. The descendants of the barbarians from Caucasia were now the very same rulers of the land. And in fact they had returned to once again continue "The Greatest War". "The Greatest War" was not simply a war of conquest, which was the primary motivation. "The Greatest War" is the war which started when the Tamahu were expelled from Africa into Caucasia. "The Greatest War" was in fact the first and longest running war for world domination. It was the world's civil war. It was a war that continues on to this day.

The inhabitants of the world are the descendants of the builders of civilization and of Africa who had survived had come out of the void to dig up the past. They were "the people" of knowledge who gave light to the world once again. They were the operators of the technology. They were the instructors to the world. Cahokia was a part and parcel of that civilization.

The notion that the great continents which composed Kemanahuac were unknown was the invention of the barbarians who came for the treasures to be found. When they discovered the secret of Kemanahuac, Anahuac, and Aztalan they perpetrated a massive cover-up to keep the truth of the land hidden.

The evidence that "the people" left behind was left in plain view for all to see. Within Aztalan alone there were thousands of pyramids. "The people" built more than fifty thousand pyramids worldwide, including that ones in the lands now known as Egypt, Sudan, Mexico, China, and the United States of America. And they built countless undiscovered pyramids in South America and Africa.

Anahuac was the name that "the people" called their land. Anahuac was the name of the Continent that lay between the two great oceans. Kemanahuac was the name given to the two great continents of the Western Hemisphere.

The origin of the name of these nations lies clearly in the African origin of the founders, Kem and Anu, the first modern man. Kem was the Cushite version of the name Ham, the son of Noah. Cush was the son of Ham, who was also known as Zeus, for whom the Cushites and "the people" take there origin and nationality. The Olmec were the descendants of Cush who kept the law of the One.

The ancient peoples of the world were fully acquainted with Cahokia, Aztalan, and Anahuac. The ancient Egyptians, Carthage, Romans, Greece, China, Japan, Asia in general, and the African nation knew of and admired Anahuac. The Europeans came to the land long before Columbus and many stayed and mixed with "the people" and especially the "the real people".

The Olmec civilization following the internal strife within the Cushite Empire became the holders of civilization and that civilization lay in Anahuac, Aztalan, and Cahokia. With the destruction of Cahokia the last beacon that burned brightly with the light of knowledge was lost. The light of "the people" was obfuscated by mankind.

CPSIA information can be obtained
at www.ICGtesting.com
Printed in the USA
BVOW11s1108171117
500684BV00001B/229/P

9 780615 313528